# RAMBO AND GIANNA

## A Very Hood Christmas

## LAKIA

*Lakia* Presents

Rambo And Gianna: A Very Hood Christmas
Copyright © 2023 by Lakia
All rights reserved.
Published in the United States of America.
All rights reserved. No part of this publication may be reproduced, distributed, or transmitted in any form or by any means, including photocopying, recording, or other electronic or mechanical methods, without the prior written permission of the publisher, except in the case of brief quotations embodied in critical reviews and certain other noncommercial uses permitted by copyright law. For permission requests, please contact: www.authorlakia.com.
This is a work of fiction. Names, characters, places, and incidents either are the products of the author's imagination or are used fictitiously. Any resemblance of actual persons, living or dead, businesses, companies, events, or locales is entirely coincidental. The publisher does not have any control and does not assume any responsibility for author or third-party websites or their content.
The unauthorized reproduction or distribution of this copyrighted work is a crime punishable by law. No part of the book may be scanned, uploaded to, or downloaded from file sharing sites, or distributed in any other way via the Internet or any other means, electronic, or print, without the publisher's permission. Criminal copyright infringement, including infringement without monetary gain, is investigated by the FBI and is punishable by up to five years in federal prison and a fine of $250,000 (www.fbi.gov/ipr/).
This book is licensed for your personal enjoyment only. Thank you for respecting the author's work.
Published by Lakia Presents, LLC.

❦ Created with Vellum

## JOIN AUTHOR LAKIA'S MAILING LIST!

To stay up to date on new releases, contests, and sneak peeks join my mailing list. Subscribers will enjoy the FIRST look at all content from Author Lakia plus exclusive short stories!
https://bit.ly/2RTP3EV

## NOTE TO MY READERS

While this book is enjoyable on its own, I strongly suggest starting with Saint and Asim for the best reading experience. These are incredible stories that you won't want to miss!

# CHAPTER ONE

## Gianna "Gigi" Auguste

### *June 24th*

"Push that shit up the court Pierre!" Bishop's obnoxious ass yelled, jumping from his seat.

I looked over at Kalesha seated in front of Bishop and she immediately rolled her eyes before looking up at him and mouthing to me, *he gets on my damn nerves*. Bishop was too into the game to notice the exchange and the fit of laughter that me, Ne'Asha, Ava, and Gabby joined in on. Jibri was in front of Bishop with his noise canceling headphones on while he read a book. If it wasn't for those expensive headphones, I knew Bishop would've kept his shit quiet. Jibri was autistic and didn't play that shit when it came to loud noises and yelling. Pierre passed the ball to his twin brother and Jamel sent the ball soaring through the air.

The entire gang was in attendance at Pierre and Jamel's AAU basketball game. Now that they were in ninth grade they were finally able to play for Saint and Asim's team. Saint trained my boys up since they were in elementary school and all of my boys were beasts on the court. They were taking after their father in the height department and were already six feet at fourteen years old. My twelve year old triplets, Tyrone, Gabriel, and Gage, were right on their heels, two or three inches shy of six feet. My ten year old triplets, Jamarion, Tyrese, and Ralph, were average height for their age so only time would tell.

With all of the kids we had with us we took up the first four rows behind Saint's team but the key person missing was my damn husband. If he was here he'd be just as loud and ghetto as his best friend, but Rambo hadn't answered his phone on the drive over here, and my texts went unread throughout the duration of the basketball game. The buzzer sounded and our entire section jumped up cheering because Saint and Asim's team won the game by a landslide.

On the average game day I'd be all up on the floor acting a fool with Bishop and Rambo but my mind wasn't here, it was on figuring out what the fuck was up with my husband. He never missed a basketball game or any event for the kids, but this was his second time this month and something didn't sit right in my spirit. Insecurities crept in last time he missed a game and I did some shit that I never thought I would do, I put an Airtag in his car so I could have his location even if his phone was off.

As everyone stood around listening to Saint give a pep talk, I was already in the Find My iPhone app, pulling up Rambo's location. The team shouting, *go lions,* and the boys dispersing pulled my eyes away from my phone. Bishop walked off with the boys towards the locker room leaving all of the ladies alone for a moment.

"I gotta run and do something really quick. Gabby, can you drive the boys to wherever y'all going for dinner and let me take your truck? I'll meet y'all wherever y'all going just let me know."

"Ummm, okay, where you gotta go though?" Her nosey ass pried.

"Please just give me the keys, it's an emergency."

"Okay, is Rambo good?" She inquired.

I nodded my head as we exchanged keys before darting out of the gym. Clicking the key fob twice in the air, Gabby's Infiniti Truck beeped in the second row. Pulling my hair up into a high bun, I was happy to be wearing my natural hair today just in case I had to knock this niggas head off. Hopping into Gabby's truck, I sped out of the parking lot, rushing across town to the hood where Rambo's location was. For shits and giggles I called his phone and this time he forwarded my ass, forcing me to mash the gas harder. When I pulled up to the address, I scanned the unfamiliar house and noticed two cars parked in the driveway and one belonged to my husband. As I got closer, I could see Rambo exit the car and follow some bitch towards the house.

Before I could think, I swerved in front of the house, tires squealing loud as hell, heart thumping out of my chest. Rambo and the woman's heads whipped around, and the nigga looked like he saw a ghost when our eyes connected through the untinted windows of Gabby's truck. I barely had the car in park before I hopped out.

"What the fuck is this shit Rambo?" I exploded, tears streaming down my face.

I knew all of Rambo's family and this bitch wasn't a member. "Gigi..." he started but I was already up on him, knocking his head like a motha fucking tether ball. Every fiber of pent up aggression went into my punches. I wanted to hurt this nigga in the worst way.

"You missed our boys game to be out with some bitch!" I roared.

"Aye, y'all gotta get the fuck from 'round here with that

shit," the bitch seethed from the porch. Her voice captured my attention and my sights were now locked on her.

"Hoe you next!" I hollered, and that small gesture slowed up my punches and allowed Rambo the opportunity to wrap me up in his arms.

"I'm finna take her somewhere. I'll be back for my car later," he addressed the woman, shattering my heart. He was explaining to this bitch, not me, but that bitch.

"Get the fuck off me nigga! Stay here with this hoe! I swear to God if you let me go I'mma kill you and that bitch," I sobbed as he carried me to Gabby's truck. Rambo placed me in the passenger seat and as much as I wanted to fight, run far away from him, take his fucking head off, I couldn't, my heart was dismantled and I felt like I couldn't breathe. I rocked back and forth in the front seat as Rambo rounded the car, willing myself to breathe as I fanned my hands in my face to produce a light breeze on me.

"Baby, calm the fuck down," Rambo begged. Hearing the nigga's voice sent me to the depths of hell for two seconds and when I came back, I lept from the seat and beat his head in. The car swerved off the road and cars blew their horns but I didn't give a fuck about anything at that moment. I didn't cease my assault until the truck careened into a ditch, sending me flying into the passenger window. My eyes closed momentarily due to the collision and when they popped back open Rambo was unbuckling his seat belt.

"Now look whatcho crazy ass did. I wasn't..."

**WAP! WAP!**

My foot collided with the side of Rambo's head and he gripped my ankle, applying intense pressure, forcing me to calm down.

"I'm not fucking cheating, Gigi! You know Kelvin had to go sit down for a minute and I agreed to handle shit for him until he gets out. It's not a lot, I ain't been away from the house much, and I been at most of the games but tonight some shit popped off and I had to handle it. Mia is one of Kelvin's lieutenants and the bitch gay and you caused a scene in front of his stash spot. That girl fuck bitches, she one of them stems..." Rambo continued speaking and everything was going in one ear and out of the other from that point on.

My mind was racing until he finished speaking. Chuckling lightly, I rubbed my throbbing head as police sirens approached. "Honestly, I probably would've preferred you were cheating with a bitch than cheating with the streets! I can't compete with that! You promised Rambo, we are too old for this shit," I responded, completely defeated as silent tears streamed down my face. "When we got married, you promised to leave the streets alone for me and the kids sake. Guess we weren't worth it," I shook my head, pulling my foot out of his grasp. I'd never been thankful to see the police in my life, but those lights shining through the window offered me a sense of relief. I could get away from this nigga without continuing the conversation. He broke his word, hid it from me, and now I probably had a concussion from crashing in a ditch. "You put the streets before me for years and now you want me to play second with eight fucking kids. No fuck that, you want me and the kids to play second now. Fuck you, I want a divorce," I monotoned just before the police opened the door.

"Are you guys okay?" The officer questioned, peering into the truck.

"My head is pounding," I answered, holding my head as the officer helped me out of the truck that was slightly lifted off the ground from the angle we landed in the ditch.

EMTs rushed over to help me and Rambo ran his dumb ass over trying to hop in the truck. "I don't want him riding with us! I want to be alone."

"Come on Gigi," he pleaded.

"Go be with your first love because I'm not playing second again."

"Sir, we need to get her to the hospital," the EMT expressed, pushing him out of the truck.

His face was filled with anguish, mirroring mine as the doors closed and I didn't understand why, he was the one who put us in this predicament.

# CHAPTER TWO
## Gigi

*Six Months Later - December 15th*

Maneuvering through traffic, my head was in the clouds until the bickering in the backseat became overwhelming. My eight boys, Tyrone, Jamel, Jamarion, Tyrese, Gabriel, Gage, Ralph, and Pierre knew how to work my fucking nerves. How I laid my fast ass down and had eight kids was beyond me. In my defense, I only got pregnant three times but my eggs liked to split so I had two sets of identical triplets and one set of identical twins. After that last pregnancy ten years ago, I got my tubes tied while on the c-section table because I wasn't about to play with my life like that. Thankfully I did too because I was in the process of divorcing my husband, and caring for eight boys in the house alone was beating my ass. I couldn't imagine adding any additional kids to this shit.

"Give it back witcho lame ahh," Pierre stood from his seat and snatched his phone from Jamarion.

"You lame, pillow talking to that bald head girl. You just ain't want me to expose ya," Jamarion snickered.

"So you was talking to Mari on the phone? Then tried to play her in the cafeteria. Weakkkkkkkkkk!" Jamel shouted into the back of the Sprinter Van.

Yeah, you heard me right, my soon to be ex-husband bought a Sprinter Van when they were all out of car seats. It made traveling easy but times like today I hated it because they had too much room to fuck around in the backseat while I was trying to maneuver this big motha fucka like a school bus driver. Pierre hurled his Nike duffle bag in Jamel's direction and that caused him to unbuckle his seat belt and lunge at his twin.

"Pierre! Jamel!" I shouted, pulling the Sprinter Van over. Pierre and Jamel were my set of twins, the eldest boys at fourteen years old.

"Come on, now she finna call pops and his mouth won't stop running until we leave his house on Sunday," Gage, one of the middle twins, unbuckled his seat belt to break them up.

I stopped physically intervening in their fights a long time ago. They were all bigger than me now, playing referee was all their father's job. Hence why he was already on FaceTime before Gage could complete his sentence. Our relationship had deteriorated to the point where I only dialed Rambo's number when the boys were into it. With the phone pointed towards the boys in the back wrestling, he assessed the situation before talking shit.

"Pierre and Jamel! Y'all fighting again. What the fuck I told y'all last time?" Rambo's commanding voice quelled the chaos in the truck. The boy's eyes darted in the direction of my iPhone with widened eyes. "Nah, don't get big eyed now! What the fuck I told y'all last time?"

"If we fight again we better jump you when we see you because you taking off on us, on site," they sang in unison.

"I'm putting my shit on now. Meet me in the backyard, I

ain't knocked a nigga head in a minute," he barked before disconnecting the call.

I wanted to laugh at this ignorant fool but I didn't want the boys to think the shit was funny. They were stressing my edges out more than usual since their dad moved out of the house. According to Rambo's mother they didn't fight like that when they were at her house with him. Either way it goes, they were their problem for the rest of the weekend.

"Now sit y'all asses down and chill out before I make y'all walk the rest of the way," I sassed, throwing the van in drive again.

The rest of the drive to Rambo's house was silent. Jamel and Pierre were probably stressing over their father's wrath while the other boys didn't want to end up on the receiving end. I turned Ella Mai's voice up and allowed *This Is* to serenade the van and drown out the silence.

"So are y'all really getting a divorce?" Tyrese inquired, annoyance lacing his tone. "We are tired of packing up every few days to go between houses. I left my MacBook at home and now I can't participate in the coding class."

Taking a deep breath, I wasn't prepared to address this question today. I loved my husband but he crossed me in the worst way. When we decided to take our relationship to the next level and tie the knot, I only asked this man for one thing. Unfortunately, Rambo only remained true to that commitment for nine years, then almost six months ago he slipped back into his old ways.

"We will just buy an extra MacBook to leave at your dads house just in case anyone forgets theirs in the future," I replied, offering a solution as opposed to an answer.

The truth was, Rambo's level of betrayal hurt and I didn't know if we could come back from that because I didn't trust him with my heart. As the boys engaged in conversation as if they didn't just show their asses while I was trying to drive, my mind drifted off to the night that forced me to file for divorce and tears threatened to fall. I fought them off though, I was tired of crying all of the damn time.

My phone vibrated in my lap as I approached a red light. Pulling it out of my pocket, a smile crept on my face. It was Harvey, a structural engineer, I met while drowning my sorrows at the hotel bar three months ago.

**Harvey: Have you considered my invitation? Time is ticking away, and I'd love to spend the holidays in Aspen with you instead of my mom and sister. I just need you to give the word.**

**Me: You know what, I'll go! (smile emoji)**

**Harvey: That means you'll have to grab some warmer winter clothes. I can swing by to pick you up tomorrow if you're available.**

**Me: I can't do tomorrow but we can go Sunday before I have to pick up my boys. I'll meet you there though, you don't have to pick me up.**

**Harvey: Perfect, call me when you wake up and we'll go from there.**

**Me: See you Sunday. (heart emoji)**

"Ma, the light is green," Tyrese called from behind me.

Plopping the phone down on my lap, I mashed the gas and followed the flow of traffic, optimistic about Christmas now. I don't even know why I stalled on agreeing to the plans with Harvey. My mom was taking all eight of my boys to North Carolina to spend time with her side of the family during the week of Christmas and I definitely wasn't spending the holidays with Rambo. The rest of our circle was going to be at Bishop's cabin in Snellville, Georgia and I didn't want to be there either, it would be triggering as fuck because me and Rambo always spent time with our friends as a pair.

We pulled into Rambo's driveway and I killed the engine, tossing Jamel the keys.

"Make sure you give the keys to your dad this time," I instructed, exiting the van.

Since we split I'd drive the boys there and leave the Sprinter Van with Rambo and take my car back home. I still resided in our marital home where all of the cars were so it was easier that way. Happy to be out of the bus for a few days, I sped away from the house before the boys could get through the door good. I avoided Rambo at all costs.

Exiting the cul de sac, I stopped in RaceTrack to grab a few blunts before I made it back home. Throwing the car in park, a group FaceTime call came through with all of the girls. Ava, Kalesha, Ne'Asha, and my younger sister Gabby were the closest to me outside of my husband and I was so thankful for them while going through this tumultuous time.

"Happy birthday bitch!!!!" I screeched into the phone once Gabby's face entered the screen.

Today was Gabby's birthday and her husband was taking her and my nephew Gideon to Italy for the holidays. As her big sister, I decided to get the gang together to party before her departure in the morning. They wouldn't be back until the New Year so this was our birthday, Christmas, and New Year celebration wrapped up in one.

"Happy birthday to you, happy birthday to you..." We all sang for my sister as her silly ass fake fanned her tears away.

"Thank you guys! I love y'all so much," Gabby expressed.

"We love you too," I blurted out.

"Oh and Asim just said he will drive the Sprinter Van for us tonight so we can get fucked upppppp and have security nearby!" Ne'Asha explained, sticking her tongue out.

"Ughhhh, I completely forgot about that part of the plan for tonight and I left the Sprinter Van and drove off in my own car," I huffed.

"Well it's my birthday so we need you to bite the bullet and go back," Gabby expressed.

"Gabby, please," I whined.

"Aht aht, it's my birthday and I want every body to be fucked up when they leave tonight."

"Ughhhh, let me go. I gotta turn around and get the van," I grumbled.

"Love you sis, see you later tonight," Gabby bubbled, batting her long mink lashes.

I ended the call on them and rushed back to Rambo's house. I had a spare key to his place just in case an emergency happened. He kept a key hook right next to the door and I prayed that he left them there so I could be in and out without seeing him.

Ten minutes later I parked my car in its previous position, to the right of the driveway so Rambo would be able to back his Benz out without an issue. I rushed up to his front door with the spare key in hand. Loud music filled the house and he was clearly living his best bachelor life over there. Relieved that the keys were on the hook, I snatched them down and swiftly exited the house.

Climbing into the Sprinter Van, I closed the door and started the engine when there was a light tapping on the window. My eyes darted at Rambo in disgust and he glared back at me. We hadn't spoken to each other in three months because Rambo's bullshit didn't stop at the fact that he stepped back into the game but that was a story for another time.

When I dropped the kids off, he was always inside and we sat on the opposite end of the gym during basketball games. No matter how upset I was, there was no denying how fine this man was. Shirtless with his endless trails of ink on full display, the lord definitely took his time crafting him. My husband was handsome as fuck with his super tall, super dark ass. Since he cut his wicks, Rambo showcased a head full of waves and when he let it grow out slightly, those waves turned into the softest curls that I used to love rubbing my nails across. We were getting up there in age, now both approaching forty-three years old, and I convinced him to remove his gold teeth and now he had a perfect set of veneers. Too bad he was flashing them chiclets in other bitches faces now.

"The fuck you doing? How you gone leave me here with the boys and no transportation?" He queried, long arms spread in the questioning pose.

Rolling my eyes, I cracked the window slightly and bit the bullet to respond. "We are going out for Gabby's birthday tonight and Asim is going to drive everybody."

"Oh, well, I'll come grab it from your crib tomorrow since I know you'll be hungover," Rambo stated, approaching the van.

"Don't worry about it, Asim will bring it back to you," I informed him, rolling the window up. Throwing the van in reverse, I noticed doofus still peering into the window.

"Watch your toes," I rolled my neck and backed up. If his foot got crushed by the tires that was his fucking business.

## CHAPTER THREE
### Kalesha Carmichael

Stepping out of the shower, I hurriedly dried my body off. Traffic was horrible picking Jibri up from my parents house, and the girls were already in the groupchat showing off their final looks while I still had a few things to do before I was ready. The bathroom door swung open and Bishop strutted in holding his long hard dick with a blunt dangling from his lips.

"No Bishop, get out," I ordered, shaking my head the closer he got to me.

"No Bishop, get out," he mocked me, sitting the blunt down on the counter. "Yo nipples got hard as soon as I walked in here, you don't want me to go nowhere. Plus I gotta give you this dick before you go out in case you be to drunk to fuck when you get home."

He was right, my kitty was purring for him as soon as we locked eyes. If you saw my husband you wouldn't be able to resist him either but then I'd have to beat your ass for trying. His low fade, full beard, and dark skinned coupled with that perfect colgate smile was my weakness.

Bishop swept me off my feet and quickly reminded me

that the anaconda he carried between his legs was the added bonus. He sat me on the double sink and I shivered as the cold counter graced my bare ass. Leaning in, Bishop wrapped his warm mouth around my right breast and swirled his tongue all around my nipple while caressing my left breast with his right hand. My head leaned back and his tongue trailed up past my clavicle until his lips connected with mine. I tasted a hint of Hennessy on his tongue as our tongues danced and he slipped his dick inside of me.

My hands wrapped around his back and I pulled him in deeper. I'd never get enough of my husband's dick. He was blessed with the length, girth, and the stroke game of a porn star; the dick was all reserved for me.

"Fuck baby, right there," I moaned after breaking the kiss. Bishop placed his hands beneath my ass and pulled me off of the bathroom sink so he could easily bounce me up and down on his dick.

"Give me all this good pussy bae," Bishop commanded, watching his dick glide in and out of me.

"I'm giving it to you, you feel how wet you got her," I talked my shit back, holding onto Bishop's neck for dear fucking life. "I'm about to cum!" I screeched, feeling my orgasm rising in the pit of my stomach.

"Wet this dick up bae. Give me all of that shit," Bishop coerced and like a faucet, I was leaking those sweet secretions as he emptied his sac inside of me. "Hollin' bout Bishop no, you wanted this dick."

He carried me out of the bathroom and into the bedroom where he laid me down on the bed, dick still inside of me. I thought he was going to give me a minute to recuperate but when I felt his dick was still hard, I knew that I would have no such luck. He flipped my ass over and I had to protest. "Do not take my shower cap off because you gone fuck up my hair."

"Girl fuck that hair," Bishop retorted, slapping my ass.

He rammed into me from behind, forcing me to arch my back. I loved rough sex and Bishop knew this, that was my kryptonite and the only reason I gave in to the second round of sex when I needed to be getting ready.

After the second round of sex my hair was fucked up and I wanted nothing more than a nap but the girls wouldn't let me hear the end of it if I flaked on them tonight. I hopped in the shower while Bishop laid in the bed finishing that same blunt he left on the bathroom counter earlier. Another thirty minutes later I was dressed and in the bathroom doing my best to re-curl my hair in a hurry because the ladies were already downstairs.

"They downstairs talking shit," Bishop entered the bathroom with a smirk on his face.

"It's your fucking fault I'm not ready, you could've fucked me before I took a shower but you wanted to wait until afterwards."

"I could have, but I didn't," he laughed, planting a kiss on my neck. "Me and Jibri are going to Rambo's house to eat pizza with the boys, plus Rambo wanna talk shit about Gigi going out. Them motha fuckas need to kiss and make the fuck up."

"For real, we used to get together and have a ball. Now we gotta decide who is going to come to what event. Plus splitting up at the basketball games is weak as hell. Even if they are going through with the divorce I need them to get to a cordial space so the bullshit can stop. She still didn't tell us what he did. Do you know what he did?" I pried.

Every time anybody asked Gigi what happened with her and Rambo she said she was just tired of his shit but I wanted to know exactly what the fuck that meant. Without further details I couldn't say whether or not they were going through with the shit.

"Nah, he ain't volunteer the information and I didn't ask. I figured he would tell me when he was ready," Bishop shrugged.

"How do I look?" I questioned, spinning around for Bishop to observe my outfit.

"Like a thot. Don't get nobody head knocked off tonight," he expressed, planting a kiss on my lips.

"You know I'm only a thot for you," I stuck my tongue out and he sucked it into his mouth. "Move," I snickered, pushing him away from me. "Not about to get me started again."

I strutted past Bishop and he roughly slapped me on the ass.

"Parents please stop," Jibri monotoned from his position in the middle of the bedroom. "Bishop, we must go because they already ordered the pizza and I don't want it to be cold when I get there and you know how I feel about reheated pizza."

"I'm ready," Bishop explained.

"Good," he turned and exited the bedroom and we were right on his trail.

Jibri was my twelve year old autistic son. Bishop wasn't his biological father, but he was the only father we recognized.

"It's about damn time! We only been down here waiting forever," Gigi sassed.

"Aunt Gigi, volume," Jibri waved his index finger in the air, before looking back at us.

"My apologies Jibri," Gigi stated, making the zipping of the lips gesture.

"Her ass still ain't ready?" Ava stepped back into the house, her elevated voice indicating that she already started drinking.

"Quiet your bubbly ass down," Bishop chastised her, nodding in Jibri's direction. "I didn't expect you to be going out with them. You are usually in the house under Saint when the rest of the ladies go out."

"It's Gabby's birthday and I usually make the time to go out for special events," Ava replied. "Bishop, you should call Saint and tell him to bring the girls to Rambo's house. They have been saying they wanted to see the boys."

"Absolutely not, Bishop," Jibri fervently waved his index finger from side to side. "Jordyn doesn't respect personal space or understand germs and I am not in the mood for that tonight. I want to relax, already praying none of the octuplets get into a fight."

Low snickering filled the living room after Jibri's speech.

"I won't call him," Bishop raised his hands in surrender and Jibri nodded. "Where is Ne'Asha?"

"We are going to grab her last since she's on the opposite side of the world. Everybody should just put in an buy an entire block and build houses from the ground up so we don't have to drive all around the world on days like this."

"Absolutely not," Jibri chimed in, heading towards the garage door. "Then the house will never be quiet. Plus me and Bishop put a lot of effort into this house and we will not be leaving it anytime soon. Let's go Bishop, the pizza."

Bishop planted a kiss on my cheek and followed Jibri into the garage. My son would never let anyone forget that he played a pivotal role in designing our home and would be the architect in the family when he grew up.

I took a brief moment to lock up the house and ensure that the security system was alarmed before we piled into the sprinter van and Gigi drove us to our next stop. The shots were flowing and I was feeling good as fuck by the time we pulled into Ne'Asha and Asim's driveway. Their house was covered in enough Christmas lights to illuminate the entire block, putting the rest of the houses to shame. Every year Ne'Asha and Asim put everybody to shame with the

Christmas decor. The lawn was covered in inflatables that were strategically placed to recreate the grinch stealing Christmas presents.

Ne'Asha and Asim were exiting the house before we could get out of the car good. "Asim come take a few pictures of us in front of your house please," Gabby requested, passing him her phone.

Asim accepted the iPhone and we all posed in front of their home for a few pictures before calling it quits. We all crowded around Gabby's phone as she flipped through the pictures.

"Oh hell nah, let me go get Allie and Chloe to come take some pictures," Ne'Asha blurted out. "He can work a camera but struggles with an iPhone. The shit is beyond me."

"Please, one thing these men gone do is fuck up the pictures," Gigi added in.

"I could've grabbed my camera and did y'all right," Asim added.

"We don't have time to wait around for that," Gigi responded.

"Next time don't even ask a nigga because y'all love talking shit afterwards," he laughed.

Ne'Asha rushed towards the house in her stilettos and returned a few minutes later with Allie and Chloe. They were Asim's daughters but their mother was barely in the picture, popped in via phone at random and rarely showed her face to my knowledge. However, Ne'Asha took on that motherly role the second she entered Asim's life, and you wouldn't know those weren't her kids if you weren't in our intimate circle. They called her mom and loved her down.

"Ma, if y'all going to have a hot girl night why is dad dressed like that?" Allie eyed her dad dressed in a black t-shirt and a pair of joggers.

"Your dad is just the designated driver tonight," Ne'Asha explained.

"Lameeeee, but y'all look cute," Chloe complimented us.

"Thank you baby," I embraced her in a hug before following suit with Allie.

"Whose phone are we using because we were in the middle of watching *Good Burger*," Allie announced, holding her hand out.

Gabby passed her the phone and we got back in position and took a few pictures that turned out perfect.

"Next time it's going to cost y'all," Allie asserted. "Have fun and be safe though."

"We will, don't be up all night either," Ne'Asha hugged the girls again before Asim walked them back inside.

## CHAPTER FOUR
### Randall "Rambo" Auguste

"Nigga, did you cheat?" Bishop blurted out, interrupting the silence on the porch.

"Fuck no nigga. I love my wife and I'd never do no shit like that. I know Gigi would've killed a nigga if I was cheating," I refuted his assumption. There wasn't another woman that could compare to my wife so I'd never put myself in a position to lose Gigi over any bitch.

"Well neither one of y'all said shit about what's going on and I was going to mind my business and let you speak on it when you ready but y'all shit spilling over to everybody else. We been planning this trip to the cabin without the kids since fucking February. We probably won't ever have another time when everybody will be kid free to go on an adult trip and now it's fucked up because y'all not coming," Bishop stated between pulls from his blunt.

"Look, when Kelvin got sent up the road I told him I would step in and handle shit for him and I did it behind Gigi's back. But man Ion wanna talk about the shit, I'm trying not to go drag her ass out of that club by her fucking wig as it is. If I'm being honest, Ion think Gigi gone renege on this shit, she gone divorce my ass and I'm trying to be strong and not show my ass about it for the kids sake but you making it hard as fuck bringing the shit up," I vexed, standing from my seat on the patio.

A nigga was scared, the look of disgust she gave me before pulling off in the Sprinter Van earlier crushed my fucking heart. Gigi never looked at me like that before and after going through her text messages I had a slight reason for why.

My phone vibrated in my pocket and I pulled it out to see Dori's name flashing across the screen. I met Dori a few weeks back at the mall. Her card declined in Footlocker while I was grabbing my kids some new shoes. On some chivalrous shit, I covered her tab and she slid me her number. I wasn't looking for a number in exchange for my generosity, I just wanted the lil girl sitting on her hip to have the shoes she picked out.

Out of boredom, I hit her up one night last week and we went out to dinner and she gave me some head in the car on the ride home. I didn't take it any further than that because I felt guilty as fuck as my seeds slid down her throat but me and Gigi were separated and I hadn't fucked nothing in nearly six months. Ion know how much more she expected a nigga to take. Since that slip up with Dori, I hadn't spoken with her and the shit I saw in Gigi's phone had me answering the phone for her.

"Wassup."

"Nothing, I just wanted to make sure you was straight. I haven't heard from you since we went to dinner."

"Yeah, you know I got eight jits so shit been hectic," I explained, rubbing my hands across my waves.

"Eight?! Like number eight? Ocho? One, two, three, four..."

"Yeah, you heard me, eight," I laughed, cutting her ass off, knowing that wouldn't be the first time a woman reacted in that manner.

"Ohhh, I'm sure they keep you on your toes because my one daughter keeps me on mine."

"Ya hear me," I exhaled. "But what's up? What you got going on for Christmas?"

"Nothing, just going to be home alone. Probably go eat at my mama house. It's my baby daddy year to have Nahla for Christmas so I don't get to spend the day with her," she lamented.

"Damn, well come with me somewhere. Where you wanna go? Name the place and we can slide."

"For real? Anywhere?" She queried.

"Yeah."

"Ummm, how about Tulum," she hesitated.

"Pack yo shit and we gone fly out by the 22nd," I assured her.

"Okay. I'm so excited," she chirped. "I've never been on a plane before so you might have to hold my hand."

"I got you, it ain't that bad," I smiled and Bishop stood up, waving his hands in front of his neck, indicating that I needed to end the call.

"Aye, let me call you back later."

"Okay, don't forget about me."

"I won't. I'mma call once my nigga leave the crib and the boys settled."

"Okay," she disconnected the call.

"Don't be caking with other bitches in front of me. You making me an accessory to your bullshit. Why don't you just come to the cabin with us instead of doing some shit you gone regret?"

"Look, Gigi ain't rapping with me and I ain't about to spend Christmas at home dolo. And I damn sure ain't about to come to the cabin to watch everybody be happy with their wives while I'm all lonely and shit. Then the women gone spend most of the time talking shit and sneak dissing me all weekend, blaming me for the divorce. No fucking thanks," I waved his ass off. "Plus I know Gigi is going to be spending Christmas with another nigga, so fuck it."

"How you know that?"

"Nah, see the only reason I'm even entertaining the young hoe is because I had Gigi's phone cloned so I can see all of the activity on her shit. She been entertaining some nigga and is going to Aspen with him."

"You real calm about this shit, a complete juxtaposition for how you reacted the last time you just thought Gigi was entertaining a nigga during y'all separation," Bishop eyed me.

"I'm letting it slide because he agreed to get her a separate room because she ain't trying to fuck. Plus he a square ass nigga, got a legit job and I spazzed out like that last time because she knows better than to be messing with other niggas we did business with or any shit like that. Get a nigga outside the city or something. This nigga not from here, he from Alabama. I ran a background check on him and he passed so I'm stepping back, letting her do her. She ain't uttered but a handful of words to me since that last incident and if I show my ass like that again I feel like I might lose her for real, but a nigga be tempted man. She was calling me unstable and kept my boys away from me for a whole month, said clearly I lost my mind. Nah, she lost her mind thinking she was gone see another nigga in my city." I vented, taking the blunt from Bishop and we both plopped back down in our chairs, allowing the silence to consume us. Ion know what had Bishop's mind running, but my mind went back to the night that really pushed Gigi away.

*Me, Bishop and Asim went to the hood to stop in The Spot, a gambling house that Bishop bought from Asim's wife a few years back. We were playing blackjack when my phone started ringing with a call from Mia.*

*"Yooooo, I'm gambling, is it an emergency?"*

*"I guess it depends on you. I just saw your wife in the hood with some chick and they look like they entertaining these niggas."*

*"Drop the location," I demanded, disconnecting the call.*

*"We gotta slide, y'all keep the money," I announced.*

*"What the fuck nigga, I'm up," Bishop questioned.*

*"They said Gigi out here entertaining some niggas in the hood," I roared, capturing the attention of everyone in the establishment.*

*Bishop and Asim grabbed their cups and trailed me out of the house. Mia dropped the location and a picture of Gigi smiling big as fuck in a familiar nigga's face. My blood began to boil when I realized it was the nigga Trent she used to fuck with when we were in high school.*

*"She over in West Tampa," I grumbled, hopping into the passenger seat.*

*Bishop pulled out of the parking lot and within ten minutes we pulled up to the location. On the ride over there I texted Gigi and told her to bring her ass outside before I got there or I was going to make her come out and she left me on read. Bishop threw the car in park up against the curb and I pulled my glock from my lap, reaching for the door. "Rambo, I'm on what you on, but we got Asim with us. Call Gigi and tell her to come out before we barge up in there and start a war with these niggas."*

*I nodded my head and placed a call to Gigi's phone that went unanswered. Laughing to myself, I shook my head and disconnected the call. "You know what man, let's slide. We are too old for this shit. I'm liable to catch a body on some reckless shit tonight."*

*"You sure?" Asim puzzled from the backseat.*

*"Don't ask the nigga is he sure, you ready to shoot it out with these niggas tonight?" Bishop sounded off, placing the car in drive and easing away from the curb. As we slid past the house I let my window down and before they could protest, my glock with a switch was*

*extended out of the window letting off shots in the direction of the house. I know it may sound crazy but it was a single level home and I purposely shot towards the roof to ensure that nobody got shot unless they were in the attic. If there was a motha fucka in the attic then that was on them.*

*"Rambo, what the fuck," Bishop fumed, swerving past the house.*

*My phone rang and it was Gigi on my line. "Brang yo ass outside or I'mma spin the block."*

*"The fuck you is with my black ass in the car," Asim argued from the backseat.*

*"Gigi, just come the fuck outside! Please," Bishop yelled in the background.*

*"I'm fucking coming Rambo. Why the fuck would you do that?"*

*"Why you over here entertaining that nigga Trent?"*

*"If I don't want yo ass why the fuck would I want Trent? I came over here to grab some weed since I'm not fucking with yo stupid ass like that."*

*"Then what you smiling in that nigga face for? Got motha fuckas sending me pics and shit."*

*"Because the nigga funny Ramboooooo!!" Gigi screeched into the phone before hanging up. Her silly ass was outside when we rounded the corner though. I snatched her ass in the car and Bishop sped off, them niggas knew better than to fuck with me. I'm on all that for real.*

"I fucked up bad that night. I been doing everything I can to get back in her good graces and it's not working. I'd do anything to have my wife back for Christmas. You know we didn't have a prenup created by a lawyer, but she drafted some shit on paper after our wedding rehearsal," I explained. Pausing for a moment, I pulled my wallet out of my pocket to retrieve the tattered piece of pink stationary paper with Gigi's faded handwriting from the inside. I smiled after reading her words on the makeshift prenup. "All she asked is for me to not slip back into the streets and I promised her I wouldn't but I fucked up. She just wanted what was best for me, they ain't making 'em like that no more."

"Then why the fuck did you step back into the game? You ain't hurting for paper."

"A nigga be bored," I confessed.

"How the fuck you bored with a wife and eight jits? It's not boredom, it's a fucking addiction and you gotta let that shit go and grow the fuck up! Get a job, start a business, or something."

"That's what I'mma do when Kelvin gets out of prison. I just gotta figure out what the fuck I wanna do."

"You better figure the shit out and quick. She going to Aspen with this nigga and the next thing you know they gone be wearing matching pajamas next Christmas."

"Shut the fuck up nigga," I groused.

A loud crash sounded off in the house and we jumped from our seats, rushing into the house. The Christmas tree in the living room was tipped over and Gage's silly ass was on the floor next to the tree. Jibri and Gabriel were asleep on the recliners and I couldn't quiet figure out what the fuck we walked into.

"I know y'all wasn't in here fighting."

"Nah, Gage's clumsy self tripped over the carpet and fell into the tree," Gabriel pointed out.

"Pick my shit up when you get up," I shook my head.

"I'mma grab Jibri and we gone slide. You better think about what I said," Bishop dapped me up.

"I'mma figure this shit out."

"Asap," he commanded and I nodded my head in agreement.

## CHAPTER FIVE
### Ne'Asha Francis

Gigi secured a section for Gabby's birthday at Kings and we were super lit. The bottles were plentiful and I was showing my ass off this Patron. Whenever I was free of my husband and daughters I was going to revert back to Ne'Asha before the family life. Finishing my cup, I stepped off the couch and joined Gigi dancing in the middle of the section. She was in here twerking like a woman going through a divorce with a point to prove. I bent over and gripped my ankles, bouncing my ass to the beat. Acrylic nails grazed my ass in my mini dress and I didn't trip because it had to be one of my girls. The liquor was hitting and I was ready to go after the quick show I put on. Plopping back down on the couch, I took a sip of water and took the hookah from Ava.

Out of all the ladies in our group, Ava was the quiet and reserved one. When we went out she sipped her liquor and smoked the hookah but that was it. She tapped my shoulder, then looked down at her wrist before tapping gently to indicate that it was time to go. My phone vibrated in my hand and it was Asim calling. Through my liquor induced eyes I corralled the ladies and led them to the exit. It was two o'clock and we never stuck around in Ybor for the club to let out because you never knew what the fuck could pop off. When we made it outside Gabby was fucked up and Asim rushed over to help her into the Sprinter Van.

"And bitch this is how you know we had a time bitch," Gigi shouted into her phone before flipping the camera to show Gabby getting carried into the Sprinter Van. "My sis might not even make it to that flight tomorrow."

"She gone beat yo ass tomorrow when she sees that shit," Kalesha cackled.

I trailed them onto the Sprinter Van, being sure to plant a kiss on Asim's lips before he took the driver's seat. As soon as we dropped these hoes off and made it back home I was going to ride his dick like a cowgirl.

"Gigi, you should just come to Snellville with us. Rambo isn't coming and we don't want you to be sitting in that house alone for the holidays since your mom is taking the boys to North Carolina," I coerced, laying my head on her shoulder.

"I appreciate the repeated offers but I have plans for Christmas now," Gigi bubbled.

"What plans do you have?" I questioned, barely keeping my eyes open because the liquor was doing my ass in.

"Just know I have plans," she informed me and the next thing I knew I was asleep.

I can't say how many drinks I had but I know I woke up in my bed naked the next morning. The blackout curtains did their thing keeping the sunlight out because the Echo Show on the nightstand read 1:18pm. Throwing the covers off of me, I went into the bathroom to shower and brush my teeth before throwing on a robe and descending the stairs, following the voices of my three favorite people in the world.

"Uno!" Asim's voice filled the entire downstairs area.

"Ughhhh! I told you to change the color or he was gone win," Chloe sneered.

"Well I couldn't pull another color out of a magic hat," Allie retorted.

Chloe rolled her eyes and I kissed the girls on their foreheads before kissing Asim on the lips.

"Nice of you to finally wake up. Did you have a good time without us last night?" Allie queried.

"Yeah, getting drunk."

"Man," I spluttered.

"Y'all focus on the game, that's why I be whooping y'all ass," Asim interrupted their interrogation before turning to me. "I made breakfast and put you a plate in the microwave."

"That's why you're the best husband in the whole wide world," I expressed, smothering his face in kisses.

I grabbed my plate and Asim won the game of uno but they remained at the table while I ate. The girls were more quiet than usual and I immediately noticed their persistent communication with their eyes. Allie and Chloe were two years apart at fourteen and twelve years old, but I swear they behaved like a set of twins. Asim was too into his phone to notice their interaction so I spoke on it.

"Ion know what y'all are saying to each other but you might as well spit it out," I encouraged them, then proceeded to stuff my face with bacon.

Chloe nodded her head at Allie then she rolled her eyes and shrugged her shoulders.

"Fine," Allie started, then took a deep breath. "Chloe has been wearing hoodies in ninety degree weather because she started getting boobs."

Asim spit out his water and looked at me like a deer caught in headlights just like he did when we went through the puberty transition with Allie.

"I told her she can't keep wearing hoodies to hide it or she gone pass out. It's hot outside."

"Chloe, why didn't you say anything? It's a right of passage, a sign of maturing, it's nothing for you to be ashamed of."

"Then why am I embarrassed and practically turning red? You don't have to tell me, I know I am," she blushed.

"That's a common response as well. Let me finish eating and we are going to the mall. I'll let y'all grab a few things then we can grab some bras from Victoria Secret. Is that cool?"

"Please remember the alternative is me taking you," Asim finally chimed in, causing the girls to snicker.

"No thanks," Chloe exclaimed. "You are already freaking out as it is."

"It's a lot, I'm not going to lie. Y'all are my babies and y'all just keep growing and lawd," Asim sat back in his chair.

"No matter how big or mature y'all get please remember y'all will always be our babies," I explained.

"We know," they sang in unison.

∽

"What about this one? I think it's cute," I suggested, holding up a black A cup bra with a small amount of pink lace covering the edges.

"Ne'Asha," Chloe fretted, snatching the bra from my hands. "Please be discreet, I already had to let that lady measure my boobs and everybody and their mama in here for this holiday sale." She wasn't lying either, Victoria Secret was having their holiday sale and I wouldn't have been caught dead in here if it wasn't for the emergency situation. I didn't enjoy coming to the mall at all during the holiday season because it be too much going on.

"It's just a bra Chloe, relax," Allie chimed in, holding up a pink bra with the PINK logo pattern going in every direction. "Can I get this one? I don't have it yet?"

"Get whatever you want," I confirmed, rummaging through the bras in the drawer that was Chloe's size. "We will just get you all of these that are your size."

"Please so we can go," Chloe spluttered.

"No, I want to look at panties."

"As long as they aren't thongs y'all can ball out," I called out.

"Ewwww, people really wear these?" Chloe frowned her face up, lifting a thong from the table.

"I saw Ne'Asha grab a pair or two before," Allie called me out and now it was my turn to be embarrassed so I was quiet.

Allie's phone rang and she pulled it out to answer it. "Chloe, it's mom," she announced and I fought the urge to roll my eyes.

Mercedes wasn't shit and probably never would be, but I kept my mouth shut about the situation and followed Asim's lead. Since it was a FaceTime call and Allie didn't have her Airpods I could hear the entire conversation.

"Hey ma," she greeted her and Chloe popped her head into the camera frame to greet her with a silent wave.

"Guess what," Mercedes chirped.

"What?" Chloe questioned, scanning some bras hanging up behind Allie.

"I'm going to come visit y'all for Christmas and I don't want to show up without gifts so what do you guys want for Christmas?"

The conversation was already pissing me off because we asked this bitch not to tell the girls that she was coming to visit anymore. Not out of spite, but out of protection. Over the last seven years since I met Asim, I could count on my middle finger how many times Mercedes came to visit the girls. However, she promised to come see them at least three times a year, once during the summer and around their birthdays. Somehow she managed to let them down every time. Hence Chloe's nonchalant response to the announcement.

I understand that shit happens but Mercedes would make these plans and cancel on a short notice. Bitch had an excuse for every occasion and I just didn't understand her behavior because she was missing out on some amazing girls.

After the fit of tears that Asim and I coached the girls through the last time, he called and requested that Mercedes not tell the girls she was coming to visit them. He asked her to relay the message to him so the girls wouldn't get their hopes up. In the event that she did show, we would make sure that the girls were available to her. Yet, here she was doing what the fuck Mercedes wanted to do.

"I just want a mannequin, so I can practice braiding her hair since Chloe won't let me practice on her anymore."

"Girl, you had me looking a mess," Chloe sassed.

"Okay, one mannequin for Allie, what do you want Chloe?"

"I'll tell you if you actually show up this time," she lamented.

"I'm for real this time."

"You say that every time and then you don't show up," Allie called her out. "If you aren't going to come please just let us know now because we can make other plans with our friends."

"I promise I'm coming," Mercedes reiterated. "Plus I remember you guys saying that your dad and Ne'Asha have taken you to every theme park in Florida except for Universal and my boo bought all three of us tickets to go. I'm coming and we are going to have a blast on the 22nd!"

"Yesssss! We love a good theme park," Allie bubbled.

"Where are y'all at? Victoria Secret? Aren't y'all a little

young to be in there? Where is your dad?" Mercedes quizzed.

"Dad is at home, mom brought us to go bra shopping because Chloe has boobs now," Allie whispered the last part and Chloe shoved her into the wall.

"Oh my God, y'all are growing up so fast and I'm missing everything. I'm going to have to buy you a bra for Christmas too."

"Please don't, Ne'Asha just grabbed every bra in my size from the PINK section," Chloe detailed.

"Okay, then let me buy you one from somewhere else," Mercedes replied. "Oh, a customer just entered the boutique. Let me sell some clothes so I can have money to spend when we go to Universal. I love y'all, see you in a few days."

"Love you too," they chirped before disconnecting the call.

They were super excited when they ended the call just like they were every time Mercedes promised them something. I bit my tongue as the girls dropped a few other items in the basket for me to purchase. While we waited in line I shot Asim a text message.

**Me: Mercedes just called the girls and told them that she's coming down for Christmas to take them to Universal. After the bad mood she left them in over summer after not showing up she better pop out this time or I'm whooping her ass. Sick of seeing them heart broken and doing them any kind of way around the holidays is crazy.**

**Asim: Chill Tyson. I'm about to call her to see what's up. I just asked her ass not to promise them shit but her ass don't listen to shit.**

**Me: I meant what I said.**

After paying for our items, I took them to Crocs to pick out a new pair then we exited the crowded mall. This was the last place I wanted to be during the holiday season.

## CHAPTER SIX
### Ava Carmichael

"Bae," Saint's voice tore me from my slumber.

My eyes fluttered open and I quickly pulled a pillow over my face because my head was pounding. Irritation immediately shot through me because I already knew what Saint wanted.

"Bae, you gotta get up with the kids because the receptionist called in and I need to help out around the gym until I find someone to cover her," he explained.

"Come on Saint, you promised," I grumbled from beneath my pillow.

"I know and I'm going to make it up to you," he promised. Frustrated, I forcefully yanked the covers off and stepped out of the bed.

I was mad as hell because I didn't drink that much while we were in the club last night yet I still felt like shit. I wanted to have a good time but I was realistic, and Saint was always on the go, so I had a very slim chance of being able to sleep in. As expected, here Saint was waking me up out of my sleep, so he could go tend to some business.

Don't get me wrong, I was extremely happy for my

husband's success, especially after everything he's been through in life. He owned three gyms throughout the central Florida area, coached basketball at the local high school and an AAU team during his offseason. However, I had to be honest, I felt like our family was being neglected for all of the aforementioned ventures since this school year started.

"I'm really tired of that same weak ass line. I'm going to make it up to you," I mocked him, storming into the bathroom and he was right on my trail. "Don't follow me in here. I don't want to talk for real Saint. You haven't been pulling your weight when it comes to the girls and I haven't complained, I understand, but you are neglecting me too now! Where is the time for the two of us? Dates, QT, and all of that shit has been obsolete since the school year started. Four whole months. You come home after I'm already asleep and leave before I can get up on most days."

"Ava, I'm not playing when I say I'm going to make it up to you. Once I replace the manager of the gym in Tampa that will run on its own again and we will be back to how we usually are."

"Okay Saint, go handle your business," I sniffled.

"Ava, I'm sorry," Saint cupped both of his hands under my chin and swiped my tears away with his thumbs. Leaning in to plant a kiss on my lips, he offered a hesitant smile. "I know I been out of pocket, just give me to the end of the day, please."

Nodding my head, there wasn't anything else I could say. Saint exited the bathroom and I got myself together to wrangle the girls solo today. I popped two Tylenol and exited my bedroom. Jordyn was now eight and Savanna was six, so I was thankful that they could entertain themselves while I laid on the couch, the only issue was they were loud as fuck. I hate to admit that my girls didn't know what an inside voice was but I was going to still ask.

"Mommy has a little headache, can you guys use your inside voices?" I pondered, placing a mug under the Keurig.

"What's wrong mommy? You don't feel good?" Jordyn queried.

"I just have a little headache. I took a Tylenol and am about to drink some coffee to combat it."

"Okay, we will use our inside voices," Savanna assured me.

I grabbed my coffee from the Keurig and sat at the dining room table where the girls were drawing. "How many days until Christmas? Daddy woke us up before the sun was up so we could go get your Christmas gift because it got lost at the post office. We had to drive sooooooooo far so I know it's special, I can't wait to see what y'all got us."

"See you talk too much, that's why daddy wouldn't tell us what was in the boxes," Jordyn shook her head while Savanna yawned and rubbed her eyes in her seat. Hearing their conversation and seeing Savanna yawning let me know they were probably tired because the sun rose around 6:40am and it was nearing one o'clock.

"You tired Vanna?"

"A little," she rubbed her eyes harder that time.

"Well come on, we can all get in my bed and take a nap," I suggested, prepared to pour the coffee down the drain.

"I'm not sleepy but I can watch Spongebob while y'all sleep," Jordyn offered. "I'll keep quiet. I promise."

"That's why y'all are my favorites."

I led them into my bedroom and we climbed into the bed. Before I knew it Savanna was asleep and I was able to close my eyes and drift off to lalaland. I woke up to the sound of knocks at the front door, but I wasn't even mad because the headache finally subsided and I felt rejuvenated. Checking the Ring camera on my phone, I saw it was Asim and the girls at the door. Peeling myself out of the bed, I went to answer the door.

## LAKIA

"What are y'all doing here?" I questioned, wiping the sleep out of my eyes.

"Uncle Saint told us to give you this," Allie bubbled, passing me a pink envelope.

After our little spat I was beyond shocked that he sent me a card. "Where the girls at?" Asim questioned, scanning the living room.

"In our rooms sleep after running me crazy," I advised him.

"Well get them up and dressed so we can take them off your hands," Asim directed as I opened the card.

*I love you and I heard you. Asim and Ne'Asha are going to keep the girls and I'm going to spend time with my wife tonight. Be ready at seven and wear something comfortable. I love you more than anything, you'll always come before everything. -Saint*

A jovial smile spread across my face and I didn't hesitate to follow Asim's commands. If he came to take the girls off my hands he could have them. "Y'all have a seat. I'll have them ready to go in like five minutes."

"And pack them an overnight bag," Asim called out from the living room where they made themselves comfortable.

"You do not have to tell me twice."

Scurrying into the girls rooms I packed an overnight bag then woke up the girls to help them get ready. Within ten minutes they were dressed, faces clean, teeth brushed, and walking out of the door with Asim, Allie, and Chloe. With the girls gone, I went back into my room and rummaged through my closet for something comfortable to wear.

I settled on a Nike joggers set to match the one Saint left the house in earlier. A cold front was supposed to come through when the sun went down and I wanted to be prepared for the drop in temperature in case he opted for an outdoor setting. At 6:50pm Saint's truck pulled into the garage while I was seated on the couch with my face buried in a copy of *The Hood's Alpha* by K. Nicole.

Hopping from the couch, I excitedly greeted Saint at the door. His handsome face was an aphrodisiac now that my attitude subsided. Although my morning rant was intensified by my hangover, those were my true feelings. The care and time Saint once provided me had greatly depleted.

"You can't be too mad anymore since you're trying to dress like me," Saint smiled, leaning down to plant a kiss on my lips.

"I'm sorry for flipping out the way that I did this morning."

"Don't apologize, I needed to hear that. I have been slacking as your husband for a few months, prioritizing work over my family and that's unacceptable," he commented, grabbing ahold of my hand.

"Where are we going?" I queried, following his steps.

"You'll see," he commented.

Chivalrous as always, Saint opened the passenger door to his Tahoe and helped me inside. I relaxed in the seat as Saint grasped my hand while maneuvering through traffic. The destination was insignificant, as long as I could enjoy some much-needed quality time with my husband. We hopped on the interstate then the expressway into Brandon. We rarely traveled this far out of the city so I had no idea where we could be going until we pulled into the Regency Square Plaza. They recently moved the Barnes & Noble from near the mall and I hadn't been in it yet. Thinking further, I hadn't been to a brick and mortar bookstore in nearly two years. I did my book ordering online but we used to frequent Barnes & Noble regularly before life got so busy.

"We got about an hour and a half before they close," Saint explained, pulling into a parking spot.

"You know I can do some damage in a few minutes," I bubbled, exiting the truck.

It was dark and the cool night air had me huddled up to Saint, giddy as hell. When we entered the bookstore, I brushed right past the book tables in the front as they rarely featured any author that I would be interested in. Saint gripped my hand as we strolled through the aisles of Barnes & Noble, the scent of freshly brewed coffee lingering in the air.

Within a matter of minutes, I gathered several books by Kennedy Ryan and a variety of other popular reads from TikTok that I hadn't explored. Saint was behind me carrying a few non-fiction books that he picked out for himself. I noticed his copy of Jeezy's *Adversity For Sale* and knew I would be reading that as soon as he was finished. Deep down I wanted to ditch out of here and go home so I could hop on his dick. There was nothing sexier than a black man carrying around a stack of books. It was even sexier when I knew he was about to buy the ton of books in my arms.

"This is all I'm going to get," I announced, my arms laden with a diverse selection of books.

"Are you sure?" Saint questioned, checking his watch. "It's only been twenty minutes."

"I'm positive," I chuckled, then paused. "Actually, let's grab a few new books for the girls while we are here."

"Bet," Saint, nodded in approval before taking some of the books from my arms. We ventured over to the children's section where I grabbed a handful of books for the girls and we eventually made our way to the checkout counter.

"Early Christmas gift?" The young cashier questioned, ringing up the pile of books.

"Nah, she won't see the Christmas gift coming," Saint bragged.

"What did you get me?" I questioned, redirecting my attention to his handsome face.

"You gotta wait and see."

"I haven't seen any boxes addressed to you that didn't involve my input coming to the house," I mentioned.

"Good, that means you in the dark for real," Saint laughed. Leaning up, I pecked his lips, excited to see what he got me for Christmas in a few days.

Exiting the store, bags in hand, I was completely satisfied with the time Saint carved out of his schedule for me. "What do you want to eat?"

"I already got that covered," he assured me, pulling out of the parking spot.

"Okayyyyy then. Books and dinner."

Almost fifteen minutes later we pulled up to one of my favorite spots and my eyes lit up. I could already taste the sauce on the wings. Licking my lips, I bounced in my seat as Saint parked in the closest spot.

"You know the way to my heart," I grinned, stepping out of the truck. It all made sense now why we drove to the Barnes & Noble out of the way instead of the one near us.

Saint grabbed my hand as we approached the Yuppi food truck that sold my favorite wings. I got the wings, collard greens, and macaroni and cheese while Saint got the catfish and fries. While we waited for them to prepare the food, I sat at the picnic tables they had under a well lit area and Saint ran to the car for a moment. When he returned, a grin spread across my face at the sight of *The Other Black Girl* in his hand. Prior to Saint's schedule going into overdrive we were couple reading the twisted yet thrilling book.

"The simple moments like this only deepen my love for you," I expressed as he took a seat next to me on the bench.

He flashed that perfect smile, his eyes reflecting a mixture of affection and playfulness. "No matter how busy I get, my love for you runs deep and that won't ever change. As soon as we can, I want to get away, just the two of us, there isn't anything I'd love more than some alone time with my wife," he replied, cupping my chin before devouring my lips. When we broke the kiss he cracked the book open and I listened to him read while we waited. I savored the simplicity of the moment that magnified the love we held for each other.

# CHAPTER SEVEN

## Gigi

"Are you sure you are okay?" Harvey inquired for the fifth time since we entered Saks.

"Yeah, I am not feeling too well, this should be enough for our trip. Anything else I'm sure I can pull out of my closet," I answered nervously.

Truthfully, I could've ran another lap in here and grabbed a few additional things but shopping with Harvey was eerie as hell, and my anxiety was through the roof. I hadn't entertained any men since I met my husband during my senior year of high school. Knowing that Rambo wasn't wrapped too tight also made me fearful of going from store to store with another man. We parked right outside of Saks and I quickly decided that this would be our only stop for the day. My nerves were too bad for this shit.

"Are you sure?" Harvey questioned again, accepting our bags from the cashier.

"I'm positive," I assured him with a smile on my face. We scoured the racks and I grabbed a few pieces and now I needed to get the fuck out of here with Harvey to ease my anxiety.

"Okay, don't stress about it too much. Anything you might need, we can grab when we get to Aspen. The quality of the winter clothes is better in the cold weather areas anyways."

"That will work for me," I confirmed, strutting through the exit.

Harvey hugged me from behind after placing my bags in the backseat and this shit felt smothering. We kissed, hugged, and went on a few dinner dates outside of the city, but being this intimate so close to Rambo made me uncomfortable. To make matters worse, I wasn't fearful for myself or worried about anything Rambo would say or do to me, I was terrified for Harvey's safety. This made me question my decision to deal with him on a more serious level. If a man couldn't stand in the paint with my husband, I probably should just leave them the fuck alone.

My phone rang and Harvey released the grasp he had on me as I ignored Rambo's call. "Our flight from Tampa to Atlanta leaves at 9:00am. I would prefer it if you let me pick you up."

"I would prefer to drive," I pecked his lips then rounded the car. Harvey leaned down into the car, peering at me as I eased into the driver's seat. Offering him a brief smile, I needed to go just in case Rambo was calling because I was within his eyesight. "See you later," I waved, shutting my door, ending the prolonged salutation. On other occasions, I thought the shit was cute, but not today.

The line to exit the parking lot of International Mall appeared endless from where my car was. While waiting in the line a FaceTime group call initiated by Gabby came through. Tapping the green button, I sat my phone on the stand so I could chat and drive at the same time.

"Y'all hoes still alive without me?" Gabby inquired once everyone joined the call.

"Of course," I smiled.

"Where you going or coming from?" Ne'Asha inquired.

"Looks like the mall, this hoe going shopping without us," Ava added.

"You better be grabbing all of us a Christmas gift or else ain't no way I'd be at the mall right now, fighting with all of that damn holiday traffic," Gabby added before my nephew Gideon's face popped over her shoulder.

"Dad said you need to get off the phone and get dressed," he ordered.

"Boy, tell yo daddy come say it to my face," Gabby waved him off before peering back into the phone. "Herc has so much planned for this trip so I probably won't be on the calls much, plus the time difference will also have us on different times."

"Girl, enjoy your trip. I love you, be safe," I blew a kiss into the phone.

"I love y'all too," she chirped and disconnected the call.

"Back to you Gigi, why you didn't tell us you were going to the mall?" Kalesha inquired.

"I went with the guy I was telling you about," I answered.

"That's what's up, have you put any thought into coming with us to the cabin for Christmas? I told you Rambo won't be there," Kalesha detailed.

"No, I told y'all I'm going to Aspen with the guy Harvey I've been seeing."

"Ohhhh, so you are really going on vacation together for the holidays? I swear I thought you were just talking shit because you were drunk and Asim was within earshot," Ne'Asha chimed in.

"Why would I do that? I'm going for real, not about to be sitting at home alone for the holidays…"

"Wassup Kalesha and Jibri," Rambo's voice caught my attention in the background and I rolled my eyes so damn hard. It seemed like every time I got on the phone with

Kalesha that nigga was over there. I thought I could escape it today since he should be at home with our boys.

"I can tell from that eye roll that you still love that man," Ne'Asha asserted with a huge smile on her face.

"I do, I just don't like his ass for real."

"Hey y'all, I gotta go! My parents are here to grab Jibri because we are flying out first thing in the morning. I'll tell Rambo you said you love him," Kalesha snickered.

"I swear to God you better not give that nigga no ideas," I vexed and she laughed before ending the call.

"Let me go too, I'm about to run over to Rambo's house while he is gone so I can avoid him while grabbing the boys," I informed Ava and Ne'Asha who were still left on the phone.

"I need to go too, this is our first time spending a few days away from Jordyn and Savanna. I'm already anxious about it."

"Don't worry, my mama will take good care of them," I added.

"I know, it's just you know, the overprotective mom jitters," Ava confessed.

"Don't let them jitters talk you out of this trip. You and Saint need some time to yourselves, to be Ava and Saint without the kids."

"I know," Ava exhaled deeply.

"I love y'all, see you at the cabin tomorrow Ne'Asha. Have fun in Aspen with your lil boo, Gigi."

"I love y'all too," Ne'Asha expressed.

"I love y'all," I smiled before disconnecting the call.

The line was still moving slow as hell but I could actually see the light that would take me across Spruce and onto Westshore Boulevard. While waiting in the car, I sent Gage a text message to let the boys know I was on the way and to grab their things. Although Gage was one of my middle boys, he was the most mature out of my pack and I leaned on him a lot. His handsome face flashed across the screen and I quickly answered the FaceTime call.

"Hello."

"Hey ma, why you ain't tell me you was going to the mall?" He questioned after observing my background.

"It wasn't a kid friendly shopping trip," I advised him.

"You got us something?" Gabriel questioned, snatching his brother's phone.

"Boy, get out of my face. Do you even have your stuff packed? I'm finally driving out of this parking lot so I'll be there shortly."

"Clearly that's a no. Y'all! Ma went to the mall and didn't get us squat!" Gabriel told the rest of the boys and I heard them talking shit amongst each other.

"We getting our stuff together ma, do you need anything else?" Gage inquired.

"You called me," I chuckled.

"Oh yeah, I almost forgot. Dad said he called you but you weren't answering. He's going to Tulum and needs his passport. He asked can you bring it with you?"

"He's going to Tulum?" I parroted him.

"Yeah, I think he's going with some girl too. I overheard him talking to uncle Bishop."

"Stop telling me your daddy business because I swear to God I'mma knock you out if I find out y'all be telling him mine," I lectured him.

"Ma, you don't have any business to tell," he scoffed and I loved that for me. If the boys knew my business they would run it back to their dad just like Gage did to me. The difference was Rambo would lose his mind and I clearly could care less. I was actually happy to hear that Rambo was moving on, that was probably our first step to him letting me do the same.

# CHAPTER EIGHT

## Rambo

### *December 23rd*

Planning this shit at the last minute was the worst thing I ever did in my fucking life. The drive up to Atlanta wasn't too bad, traffic was light and a nigga was sliding, blowing trees with my Flawda Boys playlist going at random. Even with that said, I would've preferred to fly out of Tampa instead of taking this drive, it was a stretch. Unfortunately, I planned this shit so last minute that all of the flights out of Tampa were booked up and Atlanta was the closest option leaving today. I guess everybody and their mama was gone be in Mexico for the holidays.

We arrived at the airport with a few hours to spare. Since it was the holiday season I wasn't going to play around and make any detours. Parking in the long term parking lot, I looked over at Dori who was fast asleep in the passenger seat and I was happy for that. The conversation between us on the drive quickly displayed her immaturity and I wasn't for that shit in my space on the regular. However, if her pussy was anything like that neck I could suffer through the shit during the vacation. I ain't have shit else to do, I got eight jits, so I was used to blocking shit out. After successfully checking in our bags, I led the way to immigration where the bullshit commenced.

"Good afternoon. May I see your passport, please?"

"I don't have one. Here is my ID," she shrugged, digging around in her purse.

"Whatchu mean you don't have a passport?" I chastised Dori the moment the admission rolled off of her tongue.

Frowning my face up, it took everything in me not to cuss her ass out. I know she was only twenty-one and straight out the hood but fuck, I felt like I was traveling with my irresponsible ass jits at this point.

"Well, I apologize, but without a passport, we can't proceed with the immigration process. It's a requirement for international travel," the immigration officer kindly stated.

I know he was as annoyed as me that she brought her ass in here with nothing but an ID.

"Man, bring yo ass on and get out them people line wasting everybody goddamn time."

"Relax Rambo, it's not that deep," Dori rolled her eyes.

"It's not that deep?" I barked on her, then I caught myself about to spaz in these people's establishments and I needed to fly for my boys basketball tournaments, so I couldn't end up on the no fly list. Stalking off, her ass better be behind me or she would be as good as left.

"If you knew I needed a passport you should've told me. I never been on a flight before, how was I supposed to know?"

Ceasing my stride, I turned to mug her ass and she pursed her lips. Those dick sucking lips pushed me to plan this trip but clearly they weren't worth shit when she started flapping her gums. Dori's name fit her, she behaved just like the damn fish off *Finding Nemo*. Ol' ditsy motha fucka.

As we spent the next hour waiting for our checked bags to

be located, I realized I'd probably been better off watching Friday After Next, and beating my dick for the holidays. By the time we finally left the airport I needed a blunt bad as fuck. I smoked my last blunt as we got off the interstate for the airport and a nigga was agitated as fuck now. With the luggage safely in the trunk I took a deep breath before sliding into the driver's seat.

"You getting aggy like my daddy now," Dori greeted me once I closed the car door.

Craning my neck in her direction. "Run that shit back," I urged. She poked her lips out and folded her arms across her chest.

"Nothing."

I wasn't sure if she was calling a nigga old but that shit took me back. I had to get away from this dumb ass girl before I choked her out. From this day forward, the young hoes had to stay the fuck from 'round me. Backing out of the parking lot, I wished I didn't drive up here because I would've flown my ass back home. She was lucky my mama raised me right because I was tempted to leave her ass stranded like them fuck boys on the internet be doing hoes.

My phone vibrated and a text from Gianna came through that further soured my mood.

**Gianna: Hey can you get the kids when your mom comes back on the 26th because I'll still be out of town.**

**Me: Bet.**

The single word reply was all that I could muster without sounding like a bitter ass nigga. Clearly Gianna's lil baecation with that square ass nigga was going great while I was stuck in Atlanta figuring out how to get Dori out of my space fast as fuck.

While paying the parking fees, a phone call from Bishop

came through. I ain't even answer that shit because I'd be too tempted to talk shit in this bitch face. "Can you at least look for a hotel for us to stay in tonight? Probably put you on a flight back home tomorrow."

"So now you don't want to spend the holidays with me?"

"Fuck no," I shook my head, while texting Bishop on my phone.

**Me: Can't talk right now, I'm about to pull up and grab some weed.**

**Bishop: I thought you would be boarding a flight soon?**

**Me: This dumb ass girl doesn't have a passport.**

**Bishop: (crying laughing emoji)**

**Me: And I think this motha fucka called me old. Hollin' bout I'm aggy like her daddy. I almost pushed her ass through the window. A nigga only 42! WTF.**

**Bishop: (multiple crying laughing emojis)**

**Me: Fuck you nigga! I'll hit you when I pull up just bring the weed to the car.**

With all the damn traffic in Atlanta, it took me almost an hour to get to Bishop's cabin. Easing into the driveway behind all of the cars I felt a sinking feeling in the pit of my stomach. I really wasn't spending the holiday with my people, a divorce was approaching and the bitch in my passenger seat called a nigga old. I placed a call to Bishop's phone so I could get the fuck from 'round here before one of the women saw us in the driveway.

"Yooooo." Bishop answered the phone.

"I'm outside."

"Can you ask them if their bathroom is clean? I gotta pee," she pried.

"Hell nah you can't go in there," I shot her idea down.

"She can come in, Gianna ain't nowhere 'round here and

all the ladies went to Target to grab snacks so they will probably be there forever buying up a bunch of dumb shit," Bishop responded.

"Alright man, I'm about to walk her in," I grumbled before disconnecting the call.

## CHAPTER NINE
### Gianna

"Ughhhh, this is going to take away an entire day of exploring Aspen," I groaned, disappointment lacing every syllable as I climbed into the passenger seat of the rental car. Our connecting flight from Atlanta to Denver was canceled and they couldn't reschedule anything for us until tomorrow evening.

"If you're able to arrange accommodations for your kids upon their return on the 26th, I'm open to extending our reservation for an additional day to compensate for the delay," Harvey offered, throwing the car in drive.

"I think I can make that happen," I replied, pulling my phone out to text Rambo.

**Me: Hey can you get the kids when your mom comes back on the 26th because I'll still be out of town.**

**Rambo: Bet.**

"Accommodations for the kids have been made so we can extend our trip. I'm so excited," I bubbled from the passenger seat.

"Perfect, I'm excited to spend this time with you. It'll

show us what we really could make of this thing we have going on."

My phone rang and it was a call from Kalesha. "Hello." I quickly answered.

"Since your flight is delayed and you'll be staying here overnight, come to the cabin and eat with us then y'all can go check into the hotel."

"Girl hell no," I refuted.

"Why not? You might as well. I promise the men will not drill Harvey. We will keep them in check and ensure they mind their own business."

"Yeah, bring yo ass on. Plus you said Rambo going to Tulum with a bitch, sounds like everybody is moving on to me. Plus Bishop is on the grill already so you know what that means and the sides are already done," Ne'Asha shouted in the background.

"Oh and Rambo somehow knows you're going to Aspen with another nigga, he did a background check on him and everything. So even if the men go back and tell him it won't be a surprise. If he does bring it up just bring up the bitch he took to Tulum," Kalesha rambled on while I was mortified that Rambo somehow knew my business. At the same time, Kalesha was right, that nigga was doing him to the point that our kids even knew about it, why was I so scared? Above all else, I could really go for some of Bishop's ribs, it had been awhile since he hopped on the grill.

"Harvey, remember I mentioned that my friends will be in Snellville, which is about an hour from here. They've invited us over for a barbecue. Would you like to stop by for a little while?"

"It'll be my pleasure," Harvey confirmed.

"You heard the man. *It's his pleasure*," Kalesha yelped in my ear before mimicking his deep voice in the second sentence.

"We'll be there soon and please make sure they don't eat all of the ribs."

"We got you, see you soon. Y'all drive safely," Kalesha replied before disconnecting the call.

I relaxed in the seat and got comfortable for the hour drive after setting up the GPS for Harvey. The drive was calming and before I knew it, my ass was asleep. A gentle nudge to my shoulder pulled me from my slumber. When I looked up we were at Bishop's cabin and my ass felt refreshed. The sound of a car pulling up beside us caught my attention and it was the girls.

"Get ready for the dramatics that are my friends," I warned Harvey before opening the door.

The ladies were in vacation mode, all tipsy except Ava, who I'm sure they made the designated driver.

"Oh friend he is handsome," Ne'Asha greeted me with a hug.

"Ain't he," I mumbled before pulling away from her. Harvey stood behind us with a smile on his face.

"Harvey, these are my friends. Ne'Asha, Kalesha, and Ava," I pointed them out before turning to Harvey. "Ladies, this is my friend Harvey."

"Nice to meet you ladies," he greeted them and they reciprocated.

"Not to be rude but we been drinking and the drive from Target took forever and we gotta hit the ladies room," Ne'Asha blurted out before darting off.

Kalesha was right on her heels as I giggled with Ava before trekking towards the door.

"Harvey, can you grab the bags out of the trunk? We almost forgot about them. I'll send my husband out to help you," Ava requested as soon as we crossed the threshold.

"She just said Harvey?" Rambo's deep voice echoed through my head.

I felt like the color drained from my face at the sound of his voice and I couldn't really put my finger on why. When his handsome face rounded the corner from the dining room with a menacing glare and a purposeful stride, I felt my heart drop to my ass. Within a matter of seconds, Rambo pulled his pants up and swung on Harvey, dazing him for a moment. Rambo didn't let up, he caught him with a follow up from his left fist and Harvey found his footing, swinging back.

"Bishop! Y'all, Rambo in here fighting some nigga," I heard an unfamiliar female shouting.

One glance at her and I already knew what the fuck was going on. She came here with Rambo's dog ass. The thought of the two of them vacationing with my friends sent me into a fury and I jumped on his back.

"Get the fuck off him nigga!" I shouted as Rambo stumbled back.

Harvey was caught in the corner of the door with a busted lip and a swollen eye. My weight on Rambo's back calmed him and he backed off of Harvey. I slid off Rambo's back and everyone else was making their way into the living room where the altercation was taking place. Bishop and Asim grabbed hold of Rambo before he could resume his attack.

"Nah, let me go. I'mma fuck this nigga up some more since she wanna take his side. Bringing him around my niggas. You must've lost yo motha fuckin' mind!" He spat.

"You brought that bitch around my friends!" I retorted to show him how dumb he sounded.

"Ion know what y'all got going on but I ain't no bitch," the girl interjected.

Shaking my head, I was furious as I approached Rambo. There was a part of me that was hurt to see Rambo's new conquest in the flesh. Another part that was seething that he put us in this situation, and another part that I wasn't prepared to admit before. My heart shattered when the boys told me Rambo was going to Tulum with another bitch. I knew my husband, he was fucking her and that reality crushed me. I picked up a glass vase and smashed it across Rambo's head before anyone could stop me.

"Gigi!" Saint chastised, pulling me away from Rambo as he held the side of his head that had a slight gash.

"Yeah, y'all gotta chill," Kalesha shouted.

"No, fuck this nigga," I screamed, face full of tears. "Y'all don't even know the half. Kalesha and Ne'Asha, Rambo took Bishop and Asim on a drive-by like a month ago."

Kalesha whipped her head in Bishop's direction and the look of fear that spread across his face made me feel bad for a moment but when I was irate, anything was liable to come out of my mouth.

"Don't stand there looking like a stupid ass deer caught in headlights. Is that true?" Kalesha badgered and Bishop quickly released the grip he had on Rambo and pulled his wife towards their bedroom.

Ne'Asha shook her head at Asim and stormed down the hallway towards their bedroom.

"Bae, let me explain!" He rushed behind her.

"And this is why I stay in the fucking house if I'm not at work," Saint blurted out, shaking his head.

"As you should," Ava confirmed from the kitchen, where Saint had taken her during the altercation.

With the living room practically clear, I helped Harvey up and opened the front door. "I'm so sorry I brought you here, I didn't know he would be here."

"Gigi, you not leaving with that nigga," Rambo spluttered, shaking his head, I guess to make sure he could focus.

"I'm not staying here with you and that bitch," I looked between Rambo and the poor girl who was clearly terrified to say a fucking thing to me after the way I just rocked his shit.

"You think I'm playing Gianna? I'll catch a body right

here if the nigga don't take off," Rambo explained, pulling a gun off his waist.

"Maybe I should just let you two discuss things," Harvey punked out on me and I wasn't even mad at him.

"Bishop! Asim! Saint! Somebody!" I screeched and the two closed bedroom doors that were previously emitting sounds of verbal disputes swung open and they came rushing down the hallway at the sight of Rambo with the gun in his hand.

"Don't nobody touch me because Gigi not leaving here. I'll fall out with all of you niggas about my wife today," Rambo's voice came through ice cold and I felt the shivers down my spine.

"Y'all need to calm the fuck down and talk this shit out. The beef between y'all and everybody else getting involved," Bishop complained.

"I'mma just go," Harvey notified me and I didn't argue.

The door closed behind Harvey and Rambo put his gun back on his waist. That simple gesture was clearly the signal for everybody to get back to what they were doing because Bishop and Kalesha immediately resumed their argument.

"Bae, before you get to talkin' shit, Rambo did take us on a drive-by but I wasn't aware that's what we signed up for when I got in the car. Ne'Asha, Ion think that nigga Asim knew either, he just lost his top when he saw Gigi with another nigga," Bishop explained himself as they sauntered down the hallway with Ne'Asha and Asim behind them.

Harvey's car tires squealing caught my attention and everyone else that was in the room.

"You trying to replace me with a pussy ass nigga. He can't handle you, he left you right here where you need to be," Rambo smirked, snatching my purse. "Get comfortable, your ass gone be here awhile."

"For your information, he handled this pussy just fine last

night," I antagonized Rambo. His head tilted to the side and a flash of darkness appeared in his eyes as his fists balled up. For the first time, I saw what women were referring to when they mentioned their men chest caving in because Rambo was in shambles after my comment. I could see him fighting to stifle his anger, but I didn't let up. "And you out yo rabbit ass mind if you want me to stay here with that bitch? Give me my phone so I can tell him to come back and get me!"

"Nah, she gone call an Uber to the closest hotel then take her ass home. I was never staying here with her ass, we just stopped to grab some weed from Bishop. You ain't going nowhere but to that empty room to settle your ass down."

"So what you think I'm about to do?" She sassed, throwing her hands on her hips, garnering the attention of me and Ava, the two women left in the room.

"My bad," she threw her hands up. "I'm going, Ion want no problems, can you just pop the trunk and help me with my bags?"

"Fuck no, better ask chivalrous ass Saint or Asim," I huffed, stalking down the hallway to search for the empty room, with Rambo right on my heels.

"I'mma send you some money for a room and a flight back home. Merry Christmas!" Rambo notified the girl, further pissing me off so I slammed the room door shut in his face.

"Fuck you Ramboooo! I hope you leave with that bitch!"

"Open this motha fuckin' door, Gigi!" Rambo demanded, beating on the bedroom door as I kicked off my shoes and slid into the bed.

"Come on Gigi, open the door before this nigga fuck my shit up," Bishop called out from the hallway.

Huffing loudly, I complied but I didn't have shit to say to Rambo. He might've been able to keep me here but I didn't have shit to say to him.

# CHAPTER TEN

## Asim Francis

*L*ast night, the neighboring room was vacant, but the resounding slam of the door rattled the walls and mirrors, making it clear that we would be sharing a wall with Rambo and Gianna for the remainder of this trip. Those two motha fuckas should've kept their ass home instead of bringing their beef here and spreading it amongst the couples. Ne'Asha looked like she was ready to take my head off.

"So you went on a drive-by with that nigga and came home to get in the bed like ain't shit happen?" Ne'Asha accused, pacing the floor. "Is this some shit that could come back and take you away from us Asim?"

My wife was pissed, throughout the duration of our marriage I never saw her this angry and disappointed in me. Even during her bi-weekly visits to the county jail to see me when I was locked up, she never displayed this level of emotion. Her frustration was palpable, and I realized that this situation had pushed Ne'Asha to a level of emotion that made my stomach churn. Hopping up from my spot on the bed, I pulled Ne'Asha into my arms.

"Baby, calm down," I urged, rubbing her back.

"How the fuck am I supposed to calm down Asim? Do you know how hard it was taking care of the girls without you the last time? My biggest fear in life is going through that again and now the possibility is staring me in the face."

"No it's not, Bishop promised that he would take care of everything and I trust him. We haven't heard shit from anyone and you see them niggas not stressing it. I understand that you may not be as familiar with them as I am, but if they say they handled it, I trust them."

"That's real comforting when Rambo the only nigga out there that ain't been to prison so excuse me if I don't really trust the odds," Ne'Asha sarcastically fumed, pulling out of my grasp. "Now tell me what the fuck happened and don't leave nothing out!"

"Alright man," I ran my hand across my waves and plopped back down on the pillow top mattress. The high I had from the weed we were smoking out back before all hell broke loose dissipated, and I needed another blunt bad, but I pushed those thoughts away and regurgitated my side of the story. "Thanksgiving night Bishop hit me and said he was going to gamble…"

"The night I told you to keep yo ass in the house, yeah, I remember," she cut me off then motioned for me to continue with the roll of her hand.

"It was me, Rambo and Bishop. You know that Saint don't be with that shit. I was just going to gamble," I explained, patting my chest. "Next thing I know, Rambo gets a call that somebody saw Gigi in the same hood with some nigga. We pull up and he tells her to come outside, but she don't. The nigga fake like everything straight and tell Bishop to slide. As we pulled off he emptied the clip."

Ne'Asha shook her head, disgust etched on her face. "I'm more upset that you didn't bother to tell me than anything.

Like why? Ain't you Mr. Big on communication? I guess that's until it's some shit you wanna omit."

"I apologize, Ne'Asha. I promise I would have let you know if it became an issue, but fortunately, it never did. I ain't wanna stress you out, you run a whole financial firm and that shit stress you out enough."

Ne'Asha's phone rang on the bed next to me and she had it on DND for everybody except her parents and the girls. I was saved by the fucking bell because Allie's angelic face flashed across the screen. Her attention diverted to the phone as she snatched it up and plopped down on the bed. I wrapped my arm around Ne'Asha's shoulder and pulled her down on the bed with me. When she answered the phone we were laid back on the bed with a clear view of the screen.

Allie's eyes were red and I knew that my baby had been crying. "What's wrong?" Ne'Asha questioned, sitting up in the bed and I followed suit.

"Ma just sent us the tickets and said sorry, can't make it, have your dad and Ne'Asha take you," she rolled her eyes. "The tickets are date specific and the grandparents can't do all of that walking so we didn't even ask."

"I don't know why you crying, I already knew she wasn't coming," Chloe scoffed.

"I'm sorry my babies and I know that you guys are disappointed but as soon as we get back we will plan a trip to Universal and y'all know how we get down when we go to theme parks. There is no experience like ours."

"I know but still," Allie huffed and Chloe came into the camera view, hugging her sister. "She always says she is going to come but hasn't made it in so long."

I noticed Ne'Asha's leg tapping rapidly and gently placed my hand on her thigh before taking the phone. Staring into my daughters' dejected faces I battled with myself on whether or not I wanted to present the next suggestion from their therapist since Mercedes continued to cross boundaries.

"No matter what, you know that me and Ne'Asha love you and we're always going to be there for you guys. We've already had the conversation about what you guys expect Mercedes to do based on her past behavior and not based on what you would like her to do. However, here we are again, in the same situation and I want you guys to know that you have a voice in this situation. When I get back we are going to seriously discuss the option of going no contact for a while or permanently based on how you guys feel."

"I don't care. I already blocked her from my phone, I just wasn't going to say anything," Chloe shrugged.

"I wish I was there to love all over y'all," Ne'Asha blew kisses at them.

"Me too," I added.

"It's okay to cry Allie, but once you dry those tears, remember that you have the strength to make decisions for your own well-being," Ne'Asha reassured her.

"And we are here for you, no matter what you choose." Chloe nodded, her eyes glistening with unshed tears. She was the rock between the two of them and I was happy that Allie had her for a little sister.

"I just don't want her toxicity in my life anymore." Allie dried her tears.

"And we completely support whatever choice you make, Allie. You deserve happiness and peace in all aspects of your life."

I felt a mix of sadness and pride for my girls, they were growing into strong young ladies and I just hated that their mother aided in their journey of building their strength. "You both are so strong, and this isn't something we have to discuss further over the phone. A longer conversation will be had when we return but for now, cease communication with

Mercedes, at least until we return. I don't want her upsetting y'all further while we are away."

"Don't worry dad, I'mma block her number on Allie's phone too as soon as we get off the phone," Chloe managed a small smile before changing the subject to get all up in our business about the trip. If only they knew how hectic this shit got today.

The virtual distance couldn't diminish the love and support that flowed through the screen. Together, we navigated the difficult terrain of family dynamics, making sure the girls knew that, no matter the challenges, they were not alone.

## CHAPTER ELEVEN

### Ne'Asha

*A*fter ending the call with the girls I left Asim in the room to rejoin the women. Ava and Kalesha were outside near the bonfire cuddled up underneath blankets with a blunt in the air and plates of food in their laps. Kalesha passed the blunt to me and I took a long hard pull as I plopped down in the empty seat.

Taking my second pull from the blunt, I passed it to Ava, who never smoked but always assisted with the rotation. Kalesha accepted the blunt as I rubbed my hands together to aid in fighting the cold weather.

"Bishopppppp! We need another blanket for Ne'Asha!" Kalesha called out loud as hell causing everyone to laugh.

"Girl, I could've got up to grab my own blanket," I chuckled as Bishop walked out with another blanket.

"Thank you, Bishop."

"You're welcome. Don't go too hard on my boy, he in here throwing food on his plate mad as a motha fucka," Bishop pointed towards the dining room.

"That's not even what's wrong with him. Ask him, he'll tell you," I encouraged Bishop.

"Bet," he nodded, retreating to the interior of the home.

"Well if that's not what got Asim tripping what's up?" Kalesha inquired.

"I'm ready to knock Mercedes' head off. I'm so sick of that hoe," I vented and ran down the recent events to the girls. The blunt was back in my hand by the time I was finished with the story and I took a long hard pull and looked up at the starry night sky before exhaling the weed smoke.

"Damn that's fucked up," Ava shook her head. "She's missing out because Allie and Chloe are amazing. Smart, funny and when they are older Mercedes is going to regret not being there for them."

"Oh most definitely," I agreed. "I'm just like how long are we going to let Mercedes keep showing them they aren't a priority to her. She got time to chase dick all over the country but not take care of her kids," I paused to take another pull. "Fuck taking care of them, we got that in the bag, them girls don't want for a thing. But she doesn't have time to just be there for them physically or emotionally either. Hasn't made it to one cheerleading competition, award ceremony, birthday, or Christmas since Asim got them. I'll give it to the bitch, she did pop up last year to take the girls shopping on Black Friday two years ago but that was it."

"We already knowing," Kalesha chimed in as I passed the blunt to Ava for her.

Relaxing silently in my chair, I drew my feet up onto the seat, so I was positioned Indian style. Now that I was good and high, I made up my mind that I was going to pay Mercedes a visit if she was in Atlanta while we were here. All I needed her to do was drop the location.

"What the fuck you smiling for?" Gigi pried.

"I'm about to follow Mercedes on Instagram and if I happen to run into her this weekend then it's up," I shrugged. "And y'all hoes better bail me out of jail if it comes to that."

"One thing y'all gone do is show y'all fat asses," Ava chuckled.

"And while you talking shit, I need you to make sure you keep your nose clean so you can be the one to bail my ass out. Kalesha and Gigi are liable to jump in or pop off before me," I admitted.

"And you know I'm with the shits," Kalesha took a swig from her water.

By the time I located Mercedes' page Ava and Kalesha were crowded around my phone to see what I was viewing. I hit the follow button since her page was private then looked up at Ava and Kalesha. "Relax, we gotta see if she'll even add me," I cackled.

"Oooppp, and she did," Ava snickered, staring at my phone.

My eyes swiveled in that direction and sure enough, Mercedes added me and sent a message in a matter of seconds.

**MercedesFromTheA: Damn bitch, I gave you the nigga and the kids, what the fuck else you want an outfit? Shop the boutique hoe. @ATLChic**

"Oh this hoe spicyyyyyyy!" Kalesha chortled.

"Real spicy. She has had plenty of slick shit to say over the years but Ion give a fuck no more," I expressed, watching the door to ensure that Asim was still oblivious to my actions while I typed my response.

**Me: No hoe, I just want you to drop a location so I can pull up. (angel emoji).**

The message status instantly switched to read and the bubbled popped up to signal that she was texting but then it disappeared.

"Scary ass bitch," I grumbled.

"I know, I thought we was really about to get some action," Kalesha lamented on her way back to her seat.

"Today wasn't enough action for y'all?" Ava pried and we both burst out laughing at our innocent baby of the bunch.

She was the youngest out of the clique at thirty-one years old while me, Asim, Saint, and Kalesha all graduated the same year and were thirty-three years old. Then we had Bishop, Gigi and Rambo who were all forty-two. Ava and Saint were the more mellow out of the bunch and that showed at every angle.

"And don't leave this bitch either, Gigi! We staying here and sharing a room, like we have been doing for the last three years since Bishop bought this motha fucka. Ion care if you wanna play mute," Rambo lectured Gigi as she stepped out of the house to join us.

Gigi jabbed her middle finger in his face and he gripped her wrist and pulled her finger to his lips and planted a kiss on it before she snatched it away.

"Please pass me the blunt," Gigi requested, coming straight for the blunt that Kalesha just passed me. I took a quick pull and passed it to Gigi because my good sis clearly needed it. Rambo stood at the door staring her down making shit real awkward until she looked back up at him. "Ughhh nigga, what the fuck you want? I'm not about to run off in the middle of the night."

"That's what the fuck I thought," he sneered.

I laughed hard as shit because you would've thought these two were the babies of the bunch based on their behavior. Rambo sauntered towards the side of the house with his phone out, texting his fingers away.

"Look at his stupid ass, probably checking on that bitch. Only reason I ain't drag the lil bitch all up and through here was because I could tell she was young and dumb. Thought she came up on a lick with his stupid ass," Gigi vexed.

"Lawd this is about to be a long few days with y'all two love birds beefing."

"Yeah because she clearly give a whole lot of fucks the way she biting the inside of her cheek," Kalesha called her out and she ceased her angry twitch.

"You still care, real bad," I added.

"How can I not? We have eight kids and twenty-four years together," she paused to take a pull from the blunt. "But that nigga crossed me in the worst way and he gotta feel me for real. Look at him, can't even be still he so fucking mad." Gigi ranted, never taking her eyes off of Rambo until he disappeared on the side of the house walking towards the front.

"If he left his keys in the room I'm going to take them and haul ass," Gigi informed us, standing up to leave.

"Oh fuck no, you not getting off that fast," Kalesha called out, snatching the blunt from her hand. "How the fuck you wait until you mad to tell us about the drive-by? We talk damn near daily."

Gigi plopped back down in her chair and sighed deeply. "I'm sorry y'all. I ain't say shit because I didn't want y'all to be mad at the men, I know Rambo had them into some bullshit," she paused and looked at me. "I hope you not still mad at Asim, I shouldn't have blurted that out like that. I was just so fucking mad at Rambo and wanted y'all to understand the extent of his betrayal. I'm sorry boo," Gigi apologized and I waved her off.

"You good. It was Asim's job to tell me some shit like that. If he wasn't being a sneaky nigga and keeping secrets there wouldn't have been an issue. I'm glad you told me because he clearly wasn't going to," I grumbled, accepting the blunt after she took her second pull. "He was in there trying to feel me up after we talked to the girls and shit but I ain't with it, now I'mma be stressed about that shit coming back on them. Now I understand why you been giving Rambo the blues."

"Relax sis, you don't have to worry about it coming back on them. The spot Rambo shot up was a trap house, it's my cousin baby daddy spot and Bishop took care of them. Nobody gone say shit, nobody got hurt."

"Well that's good to know," I relaxed in my seat as Kalesha passed me the blunt.

"Not you was just on Asim ass about jail and you preparing for your own mugshot," Ava shook her head.

"What happened? What did I miss?" Gigi perked up after Ava's comment and we took a brief moment to fill her in while I checked to see if Mercedes replied and she still hadn't, clearly she was pussy. My eyes caught a glimpse of a car pulling into the driveway and I squinted my eyes to make sure I wasn't tripping.

"Is that your boo Harvey's car?" I squinted, unsure if I was high, confused, or what.

Gigi's head snapped around in that direction and she stood to her feet. "You think that preppy motha fucka is the type to spray the block? Because please let me know, so I can hit the floor."

"Girl shut the fuck up," Gigi snickered. "That can't be him. I don't think he'd be that dumb to come back."

# CHAPTER TWELVE

## Rambo

***Ten Minutes Prior***

All that shit I was spitting to Bishop a few days ago about stepping back and giving Gigi space went out the window when I saw her walking close to that nigga. That *out of sight, out of mind* shit was the realest shit they ever quoted because the moment they were in my peripheral, smiling like a happy couple, the beast roused within. As hot as I was with Gigi, I couldn't put my hands on her, but the nigga who touched a treasure that belonged to me had to get it.

If seeing Gigi standing next to another nigga wasn't enough, my knees almost buckled when she admitted to fucking him. I hadn't even fucked nobody since we split up, deep down inside I was holding out hope that we would work this shit out.

*He handled this pussy just fine last night,* was a phrase that would haunt me until my casket dropped. Her angelic voice spitting those venomous words set my veins on fire. I felt the tension gripping my muscles, my fists clenched so tightly that my nails dug into my palms, leaving indentations. The room seemed to shrink, and the air grew heavy with my suppressed rage. Every fiber of my being craved a release to silence the haunting echoes of her words. The angel on my shoulder won the battle, if my emotions spilled out in the form of rage, I'd lose my wife forever. Willing myself to breathe, I counted in my head until Gigi spoke again.

Although she let me in the room, she ignored everything I said to her, and pretended like I didn't exist until she went outside. The kiss I planted on her knuckle was the closest feeling of affection that I'd experienced with my wife in nearly six months. I missed her bad as fuck but she was determined to give a nigga the blues.

Stalking off into the darkness towards the side of the house I pulled Gigi's phone out of my pocket and went through her shit since she wasn't smart enough to change her passcode. After seeing Gigi planning the trip with the nigga I stopped reading her text messages. I wanted to avoid seeing some shit I didn't wanna see. Plus I was tired of seeing her call me all types of fuck niggas when she was texting the girls. The only text thread I cared to go through was between her and that nigga Harvey.

**Harvey: Are you okay? I don't want to call the police but if you don't at least check in I will send them there to do a wellness check for you.**

"Pussy ass nigga," I mumbled to myself before responding to his text from five minutes ago.

**Me: I'm straight, come pull up on me. I'm not trying to stay here.**

**Harvey: Are you sure that's safe? Should I bring the police?**

**Me: It's safe. We don't need the police involved. Just come get me. He's in the crib sleep and I'mma be on the left side of the house. Cut the lights off when**

**you get on the street and pull to the side. I'mma come out to you.**

**Harvey: Okay, I checked into a hotel not too far from there, give me like ten minutes. I was already out grabbing food so I'm not far at all.**

**Me: Bet.**

I moved to the other side of the house where the driveway continued behind the house for the boating dock. Lying in wait, Gigi's words continuously cycled through my thoughts, fueling the malevolent motha fucka that I buried when I stepped out of the streets. As promised, the nigga pulled up to the house, calling Gigi's phone in the process and I ignored the call. He continued driving, lights off, slowly rolling it into the darkness until he reached the side door.

Harvey stepped out of the car and into the darkness making my plan easier to execute. "Gigi," he whispered, approaching the side door.

I crept up behind Harvey and put his ass in a chokehold. My grip tightened around his throat and a desperate gasp escaped his lips, as he fought against my grasp. That only made me tighten my biceps and forearm around his neck, leaving him wheezing loud as fuck. His struggle for breath filled the distance and Kalesha's nosey ass peeked around the corner.

"Oh my God! Y'all it was Harvey's car! Rambo about to kill him," she snitched.

Gigi rushed around the corner first, pissing me off more. My furious gaze landed on her, our eyes locked and she knew not to pull none of that shit she did earlier. "Rambo! Get the fuck off of him!" She screeched.

"You fucked this nigga, his blood is on your hands," I replied, flashing a cold grin.

"Bishop! Asim! Saint! Some fucking body come get this crazy ass nigga!" Gigi shouted and they came rushing out the side door. When they laid eyes on Harvey confusion filled their faces.

"If he came back he wanted the smoke," Bishop interrupted the deafening silence.

"Facts, plus we way out here, easy to get rid of his body and his car."

"Rambo..."

"Nah, don't call my name now," I cut her off. "Throughout this separation I ain't even fucked nobody else. Clearly a nigga is fertile as fuck and with my luck, the vasectomy would fail me and I'd get a random bitch pregnant. I knew I'd never get my wife back if I fucked around and made an outside child so I kept my dick in my pants. But you... you fucked this square ass nigga."

"Rambo, I didn't fuck him I swear I didn't. I put that on our kids. I just said that shit to make you mad since I know you was fucking that hoe."

"I didn't fuck her, she sucked my dick and that was it," I argued. "Don't put no lies on my jits, Gigi! Not to save this weak ass nigga."

"I wouldn't do no shit like that! My word is my bond and I've never lied to you, never betrayed you, but can you say the same?" She teared up, tugging at my heart strings as she wiped at her eyes.

I instantly felt that dark feeling slowly dissipate. Gigi didn't play about our kids, she wouldn't lie on them like that. I felt my faith restored with those two sentences and released the grip I had on Harvey. He tumbled to the ground, leaves cracking beneath him as he gasped for air.

"This is why you need to stay the fuck from 'round other niggas wives. She lied on yo dick and almost made me snatch yo life," I grumbled before stalking back into the house and pulling Gigi inside behind me. "Any nigga I see you with can take a dirt nap, you better stop fucking with me."

# CHAPTER THIRTEEN

## Gianna

Rage filled Rambo's eyes but I picked up the hurt in his tone when he spoke. Seeing Rambo with that young hoe, hurt my heart more than I was even prepared for. I still loved my husband, I just needed him to choose his family first. Stomping into the room with Rambo leading the way, I didn't have any idea where we were going from here.

"Ion know why you stomping around this bitch. You the one lied on yo pussy," Rambo shrugged, snatching his blunt and weed from the nightstand to roll a blunt.

I watched patiently as he rolled the blunt because my husband was an expert. This was our first time being this close in months and observing him lick the edges of the blunt had my kitty tingling. *Maybe I should've fucked Harvey so I wouldn't be so turned on when I was supposed to be pissed.* I thought to myself. The moment Rambo was done with the blunt I snatched it from his hands and lit it to take a long hard pull. Consumed with my thoughts, I was on my third pull before he snatched it away from me. "Come on, you hogging my shit."

"What's mine is yours and what's yours is mine," I

expressed, plopping down on the bed, staring up at the ceiling. My stomach emitted an obnoxious rumble because I hadn't eaten since breakfast.

"Here, let me fix you a plate," Rambo stated, passing me the blunt.

I kept smoking until he returned with a plate piled with everything my inner fat girl desired and a bottle of water in his hand. We exchanged items, the blunt for the plate, before he reclaimed his seat. I finished half of the blunt so I was super high and hungry. While digging into my plate I stole a few glances at my husband's side profile.

There I was, referring to him as my husband again because my heart was beating for him. I wanted him to pull me close, tell me that he would leave the streets alone and that everything would be okay. He finished off the blunt while I continued eating and stood from the bed, pulling his shirt over his head. Stifling the deep exhale I wanted to emit after seeing him shirtless, I openly stared at the muscles in his back as he exited the room.

I finished my plate and went to the kitchen to toss my trash and see where the fuck Rambo was going. Everyone else was outside, probably talking mad shit about us but I didn't give a damn because Rambo wasn't with them. When I spun around from staring out of the kitchen window I spotted Rambo sauntering through the front door with his suitcase, reminding me that my shit was still in Harvey's trunk.

"Did you really go outside in the night air with no shirt on? It's like sixty degrees."

"I'm straight," he shrugged. "I took off my shirt before I remembered I couldn't take a shower without a change of clothes. Plus you gone need one of my shirts or something to sleep in."

"Yeah," I commented, trailing him back into our bedroom.

He stepped out of his pants and tossed them into his laundry bag with the rest of his dirty clothes. No matter how mad I got, Rambo was irresistible and that's why I kept my distance during this separation. I enjoyed sex just as much as the next bitch and the toys could only provide so much sexual gratification. There was nothing like a pair of strong hands caressing every inch of your body and a pair of passionate lips laying tender kisses. My ass was standing there in a puddle and I turned on the tv to distract myself, attempting to resist the urge to join him in the shower. Looking away as he swaggered into the bathroom with his Versace boxer briefs, I shuddered once he was out of sight. Rambo knew what the fuck he was doing and I wasn't going to fall for his bullshit.

That was until he exited the bathroom with his dick swinging freely because he forgot his towel on the bed. My body calmed down during his absence but I was heated again. This was my first time in his proximity for an extended period of time, and my pussy was screaming for his ass while my mind and heart were still looking to punish him.

Hopping from the bed, I snatched the towel and stomped into the bathroom. I took a lengthy, steaming shower, allowing the scalding water to cleanse away the lustful thoughts, drama, and stress. If he wasn't in the next room I would've played with my own pussy but I couldn't give him the satisfaction of knowing the effect he still had on me. With a clear mind, I exited the shower and dried off and went looking for some of Rambo's clothes to throw on.

When I stepped out of the bathroom Rambo was relaxed on the bed in nothing but his boxers, gliding his thick tongue across another blunt. That visual was like an aphrodisiac and I couldn't resist my urges, I needed to be licked like his swisher. Sauntering over to his spot on the bed, he offered an apprehensive glance until I dropped my towel and a huge grin spread across his face. Like an animal in heat, he released his grip on the blunt and pulled me onto the bed with him, devouring my lips. The fire brewing between us was inevitable and I eagerly surrendered to the familiarity of our bond.

We were both immersed in one another, rediscovering every part of each other's body through deliberate and tender touches. Rambo knew I loved physical touch and he ensured that his strong hands caressed every inch of my smooth skin before traveling south. I gasped as his hands finally made their way between my legs and he gently massaged my pussy, cupping it with his big hands. The sensation ignited an insatiable fire deep within my core, causing me to grind into Rambo's hand. His tongue found its way down my neck and to my nipples. I was instantly lost in pleasure, my desire for him taking over completely once he slipped two fingers inside of me.

"Fuck Rambo," I moaned.

Suddenly he pulled away, leaving me breathless and craving more. He smiled devilishly as his eyes surveyed every inch of my body before reaching up to caress my face. "I'm 'bout to make you forget all that bullshit and remember why you love a nigga." His voice was low and seductive, sending a wave of heat through my body. I believed every word he said and I leaned down to kiss him again.

He wrapped his arm around my back and flipped us over. Abandoning my lips again, Rambo traveled further south with his tongue, leaving a trail of fire along my warm skin. My back arched as his tongue flicked across my clit, giving me exactly what I yearned for. After a few sensual licks, Rambo dipped his tongue inside of my pussy, exploring me in the most intimate way. Trailing his skillful tongue back to my clit, he swirled around a few times while gliding his fingers into my pussy.

"Oh my.... Rambo! I'm about to cum! Shit baby," I

screamed, feeling an orgasm rip through me. My nails ran across his scalp as I tried to fight Rambo off but he sucked me right through the orgasm, causing me to moan louder than I would've liked to in a house full of people.

The soft yet passionate sensation caused my body to pulsate with pleasure and I erupted into a world of unimaginable heights as a second orgasm hit me almost immediately after the first one. Rambo pulled away and grinned cockily before pressing his weight against mine and gripping onto my hips. He entered slowly, as if savoring every inch that he thrust into me and I was appreciative because my bout of abstinence had me wincing slightly as if I was a virgin again.

"This pussy was waiting for a nigga, she gripping a nigga like she don't wanna let go. Ion know why you playing, can't nobody beat this pussy down like yo husband can. She don't want nothin' else but this dick," Rambo expressed as he increased his pace.

My hands ran up and down his back to stifle the pain that peaked through the pleasure. Once my body readjusted to his size, I thrust my hips towards him and he released the grip he had on my hips and leaned down until he was hovering directly over my face. "Fuck me like that Gi," he instructed and I loved when he gave me orders in bed. His lips intertwined with mine as he played with my clit and I was done for. He met my thrusts with his own, our skin slapping resounded in the room. I felt my orgasm building from deep inside me and Rambo knew. "I feel that pussy twitching, cum for me bae. I'm about to cum too," he announced, breaking our kiss as he drilled inside of me, lifting my leg giving him better access to my clit and deeper strokes.

I yelped in pleasure as an intense orgasm shot through me and my pussy tightened around his dick, pulling the nut out of him. I felt his nut shoot out of him before he pulled out and collapsed on the bed next to me. He reached over and caressed my thigh gently before sleep consumed me. I needed every stroke, lick and orgasm that he gave me.

When I woke up in the morning we were in the same position, a heap of sweaty mess. I shook him awake so we could take a shower. His frazzled expression when he woke up was always funny to me, Rambo was a confused mess when he didn't get enough sleep. "Let's take a shower so I can wash the sheets. It smells like they already cooking breakfast."

"Alright," he blinked rapidly, before sitting up in bed. "I love you, Gianna."

"I love you too," I nodded, easing out of the bed and making my way to the bathroom.

We showered together and of course he fucked me silly, leaving no room for conversation. Nearly two hours later we were dressed and joining everyone at the table for breakfast. I was unfortunately wearing a pair of his basketball shorts and t-shirts since my luggage never made its way out of Harvey's trunk.

"You had a better night than the rest of us," Ne'Asha snickered, shoveling grits onto a plate. We were all moving around the kitchen placing food on plates and I was done before everyone else so I was standing around picking off my plate, dreading the seating arrangement at the table.

"I needed it more than the rest of y'all too," I expressed.

"You might be right because one thing Bishop gone do is give me a tuneup at the end of the night. Whether we on good terms or not. I don't know how you lasted six months," Kalesha shuddered.

"Niggas just don't excite me like that and my husband don't deserve no pussy. That was for my own needs last night," I shrugged.

"Damn, it's like that?" Rambo questioned from the dining room.

"Absolutely," I laughed.

He waved me off until we exited the kitchen. All of the women placed plates in front of their husbands while Rambo looked at me in confusion.

"Boy, I wasn't playing. Just because we fucked last night don't mean we are miraculously repaired. I was horny and you know I love the stuff you do," I flicked my tongue at Rambo and he glared at me, but I could care less.

## CHAPTER FOURTEEN
### Ne'Asha

"It's Christmas Eve, you niggas gone have some holiday cheer and stop the bullshit, or get the fuck up out of here," Bishop threatened Rambo and Gianna, interrupting their heated stare down. "You had Kalesha and Ne'Asha beefing with us momentarily because y'all shit ain't together. We ain't going out like that on Christmas Eve. Get along for the next forty-eight hours without your bad ass jits. Let's enjoy the motha fuckin' weekend."

"Period," Kalesha chimed in to support her husband, making it clear with a sloppy kiss. "We will be playing couples games tonight and drinking liquor. It will be a vibe. This is probably the first Christmas in years that none of us will be up wrapping gifts and putting shit together and we are about to enjoy it... kid free."

"Amen, with all the kids between us, this is a Christmas miracle in itself," Ava added in.

I nodded in agreement as my phone vibrated on the table. Rambo silently stood from his chair and went into the kitchen to wash his hands and make his own plate.

"You might've messed up. Now he gone withhold dick for

the rest of the trip," Kalesha laughed, as we all watched Rambo fix his plate mad as hell.

"That's on him, I had enough to last me another six months," Gianna clarified.

I was happy that the disgruntled couple garnered everyone's attention so Asim missed the silent grin that spread across my face at the message that popped up on my notification screen.

**MercedesFromTheA: I'm not hard to find, bitch you don't be looking. Go play in traffic. (crying laughing emoji)**

Then it hit me, the bitch owned a boutique. I clicked on her profile and the boutique was tagged in her bio and the address to **@ATLChic** was pinned to the top of the page. I screenshotted the address and finished breakfast in a great mood.

"We going into the city to grab a few things. What y'all getting into?" Saint questioned the women.

"We are going to do a little shopping as well," I chimed in.

"Who the fuck is *we*? Ain't nobody about to be fighting for their life in no mall on Christmas Eve," Gianna grumbled, her pretty face screwed up. "Plus, I don't even have clothes because somebody..." she rolled her neck in Rambo's direction.

"Bring that nigga up and see don't I go hunt him down for your luggage and to finish the job. Ion give a fuck if you didn't fuck him, he was too close to mine."

Gianna sighed deeply before positioning both of her middle fingers in front of his face.

"Relax Gigi, we are going to a little boutique and we are about the same size so you can throw on one of my jogger sets. They are a little big on me so they should be perfect on you."

"Thanks pooh, maybe I'll find an Atlanta nigga since

Rambo don't want me fucking with no niggas in the city," she teased as he sat next to her, placing his food on the table.

His eyes quickly shifted towards Gianna, and the lethal gaze he shot her made me fearful for her life. After a few seconds lapsed Gianna tilted her head to the side and she mugged him with an equally menacing stare. Rambo suddenly reached out, gripping her neck and my adrenaline immediately started pumping, he was about to choke her ass out before I could eat my bacon. All of the men shifted in their seats, ready to pounce and tear them apart then Rambo did something that none of us expected, he tongued her down.

Rambo's tongue worked its way around her mouth and Gigi nastily kissed Rambo back while he held that grip on her neck. The intensity of their kiss was like a storm brewing between them, a wild clash of passion and danger that left us all stunned. He was kissing Gigi like Melvin kissed Jody's mama on *Baby Boy* and the shit was equally as erotic. I needed to look away but I couldn't revert my eyes back to my plate until Rambo released the grasp on her neck and ceased the kiss. I was holding my breath with Gigi, wondering what was going to happen next.

"You talking all that shit but if you in my presence you know I can touch that pussy when I want to," Rambo cockily asserted. Gigi took a deep breath and opened her mouth to retort but Rambo cut her off. "Say I'm lying and I'll take you in that room and prove my point, everybody gone here you moaning in this bitch. Stop playing with a nigga, Gigi."

She closed her mouth and refocused her attention on her breakfast.

"Bae, kiss me like Rambo just did Gianna, I'm trying to have soaked panties at the table too," Kalesha blurted out. Bishop obliged, tonguing his wife down and I refused to watch them because they were always all over each other no matter who was around.

The rest of breakfast was uneventful and I was thankful for that. I had asses to beat today. While the men got dressed and left for the mall, I relaxed so I could lay out my plans for the day with the ladies.

"Soooooo... that bold bitch told me where she is going to be today." I announced, watching the men disappear down the street.

"Who?" Ava inquired.

"Mercedes, Allie and Chloe's mama. Keep up, Ava," I laughed.

"So what's up, what we finna do?" Gigi snapped her neck in my direction.

"She extended the invitation and I don't want to disappoint," I expressed, pulling my braids up into a high bun before exiting the cabin.

"Oh my God, y'all was for real," Ava panicked, last to walk through the door.

"Yeah girl, you can just be the driver. You don't have to get out of the car if you don't want to," Kalesha explained, tossing her the keys to the rental car.

"It's actually not an option. You are not allowed out of the car. If troll pull up, just drive off. We gone need somebody to bail us out without the hassle," Gigi instructed, passing Ava a card as we trekked across the grass to the car. "It's Rambo's card so there is no limit."

"I know that's right," I chirped, hopping into the passenger seat.

Mercedes' boutique was in Decatur, about forty minutes from our location and Ava took her sweet time getting us there. But when we arrived, I stepped out of the car, checking my high bun for security. Kalesha and Gigi exchanged words with Ava as I approached the door. Seeing her smiling, while staring down at her phone made my blood boil, the same phone she couldn't seem to use to call her daughters on a consistent basis. I couldn't imagine going a day without talking to Allie and Chloe and they weren't even biologically mine. It took a special kind of motha fucka to move like this bitch does.

As I entered, the door chimes jingled merrily, alerting Mercedes to a patron in her beautifully decorated boutique. She looked up from her phone with a welcoming smile until our eyes met.

"Oh you a bold hoe," she spoke, face contorted. Mercedes tossed her phone onto the counter, stood up, and raised her hands in a shrug, signaling a sense of inquiry. "So wassup?"

I ain't have no rap for the dead beat bitch. Darting across the pretty pink floors, I reverted back to the old Ne'Asha that didn't mind popping a bitch in her mouth. As soon as she was within arms reach, I threw a punch; it connected with a crack across Mercedes' jaw. She stumbled slightly before charging at me full speed.

"Bitch!" She exclaimed before we went at it.

We exchanged blows, neither of us backing down but I was moving off of pure adrenaline so any punch she landed didn't phase me. Mercedes couldn't say the same as she stumbled into a rack of clothes, knocking hangers to the floor. Metallic clatter echoed through the small space as I pounced on Mercedes, throwing incessant punches that landed on her face.

"Beat that ass, Ne'Asha!" Gigi's loud voice filled the boutique.

Crop tops and dresses cascaded down, adding chaos to the confrontation. Mercedes threw her hands up, attempting to block my blows, no longer fighting back, she was focused on protecting her face.

"Get off of her, I called the police!"

I heard a voice yell from the back of the boutique, but I didn't give a fuck. This ass whooping was long overdue. If I could've snatched this bitch up through the phone it would've been done years ago. The first time she crushed Allie and Chloe's spirit with her absence, it took everything out of me to be the bigger person. Unfortunately Mercedes' luck ran out today and her anger couldn't possibly match mine. My arms didn't stop swinging until I was being pulled in multiple directions. It took Gigi and Kalesha to get me off Mercedes ass.

"Now don't ever call my girls and promise them a fucking thing again! They deserve so much more than a trash ass bitch like you!" I screamed so loud with motherly rage, releasing years of pent up frustration.

Mercedes laid there helplessly, not expecting the passion in my voice to be this immense. I got the sense that she realized her ass was dead wrong as her bloody lip trembled but we'd heard the repeated apologies after her bullshit, I didn't have an ounce of sympathy for her ass. Snatching my arms away from Kalesha and Gigi, I flipped over a table covered in accessories, sending them flying over Mercedes and the rest of the boutique. The door chimes sounded and I refocused on the front door where Ava stood.

"Come on y'all! I hear police sirens," Ava panicked.

Fueled by the repercussions of the law, we sprinted towards the door, leaving Mercedes and her scary ass employee behind.

Jumping in the car, Kalesha took the driver's seat this time because she knew the area better than the rest of us since her and Bishop brought Jibri to the cabin once a month. My chest heaved as we pulled off, and I examined my throbbing knuckle, noticing a small amount of blood.

"The way Ne'Asha was throwing them hands, I know her army husband taught her how to fight," Kalesha cackled.

"Nah, I'm an only child so I was in cheerleading for my mama and taekwondo for my daddy growing up," I chuckled.

"You think she gone call Asim?"

"Nah, she blocked after that bullshit she did. We decided to cut off communication on our end for a minute."

"No matter what, don't let her steal the joy in your household. My sperm donor was a fuck nigga too but my mama's husband, my dad is the most amazing man, and I'm so thankful to have him. The overwhelming emotions I get about my dad, that's how Chloe and Allie are about you. Kids are resilient, they unfortunately have no choice but to be," Gigi expressed, rubbing my shoulder.

"Yeah, fuck that hoe. You tapped that ass now let's go have a drink so we can act natural when we get back to the cabin. Don't need them niggas in our business," Kalesha added in.

"Please stop for mimosas," Ava dramatically requested, causing everyone to laugh.

## CHAPTER FIFTEEN

### Rambo

"Why the fuck we gotta come down here with all this fucking traffic and shit?" Bishop questioned from the driver's seat.

I should've drove my own shit so these nosey ass nigga's didn't have to be in my business. Unfortunately, my destination was in downtown Atlanta and it would be hit or miss if I could grab a parking spot without a hassle, especially this time of year. Hence, why I was forced to hop in the whip with the fellas.

Although the entire group knew me and Gigi were going through it, I ain't vent to them often. The last thing I needed was them repeating some shit to their wives because then they'd definitely run it back to Gigi. Navigating through the mess I created in my relationship was a lot harder than I expected. After last night, I thought I cracked the ice from around her frozen heart and we could go from there, but the way she played me at the table let me know that I had more work to do. Either way it goes, we were leaving this bitch together. Ion give a fuck if I gotta handcuff Gianna to me and toss the key, our separation was a wrap. That moving on shit was dead.

"Just pull up here and I'mma run in and out real quick. I ain't ask you niggas what y'all was getting out of the stores," I retorted.

"Nigga, we was in the Hallmark store buying gift bags and that paper shit, wasn't nothing to tell," Bishop argued. "You had us drive thirty minutes out the way, we could've been back in the crib and out this dumb ass holiday traffic already."

"Oh shit, you getting Gigi jewelry?" Asim cut in, noticing where we were. "Damn, I gotta step my game up then."

"You know I gotta come super hard this year. I'mma be right back," I explained, opening the door to the Suburban.

"Nah, this nigga trying to show us up. I gotta grab my wife something too," Bishop killed the engine in front of the boutique jewelry shop in Downtown Atlanta.

I hadn't been here since me and Gigi came to shop for her first engagement ring and a sense of nostalgia consumed me.

*We just found out Gigi was pregnant with Jamel and Pierre and I took her on a quick getaway. Taking quick trips out of the city was our thing since we met. However, we knew that shit was about to come to a halt with two jits on the way. From the moment we found out she was pregnant, I promised we would get a lot of traveling accomplished before her doctor banned her from flying. Hearing that we were having twins and there would be an increased risk of complications and early bedrest pushed me to start planning our trips ASAP.*

*First stop was Atlanta for three days, New York for a week, then Houston for a week, then back home so I could make sure that Bishop was straight. It was our final day in Atlanta and we were downtown headed to this jeweler that Gigi followed on Instagram. He iced out a lot of celebrities and Gigi just had to have a piece from him before we left. She squeezed my hand as Ziggy, the owner of the store, slid a diamond tennis bracelet up her right wrist. That nigga was grinning hard as fuck, probably counting the dollars he would make off of me.*

*"I love it," she bubbled, placing her right hand on her shoulder and admiring the diamonds glistening on her wrist in the table top mirror.*

*"We gone take that too," I explained because I already swiped my card for a few Rolex watches for myself.*

*He nodded his head and scurried off. These fancy motha fuckas had security near the exit, champagne on deck and Gigi was enjoying the experience. Although Gigi couldn't drink, she had them pour her water in the champagne glass so she could drink and take pictures for her Instagram. While we waited for Ziggy to return, I glanced in the display case and a white gold heart shaped diamond ring caught my attention. It was extra and beautiful just like Gigi. I looked between the ring and Gigi a few times and decided that today was the day. She completed a nigga, I loved everything about Gigi. Her slick ass mouth, the way she loved me and the people who were special to her. My mean ass mama loved Gigi from the first day that I introduced them to each other and I couldn't see myself with anyone outside of her.*

*"Aye Ziggy, let me see this right here," I called out, capturing Ziggy and Gigi's attention. She stopped entertaining her Instagram and strutted her fine ass in my direction to be nosey.*

*"What you see now, bae?" She inquired.*

*"You gone see," I explained.*

*Ziggy approached from the opposite end of the display case grinning big as fuck. "What you looking at, my man?"*

*Gigi went back to texting on her phone and I was grateful for the distraction as I pointed at the ring that fit her loving personality perfectly. "Good choice," Ziggy nodded feverishly as he extended the extravagant piece of jewelry in my direction.*

*"What is it?" Gigi glanced back up at me as I dropped down on one knee. Never one for long speeches, I grinned up at her, gold teeth glistening under the bright lights.*

*"Will you marry me? I want you to be mine forever, Gigi."*

*"Yes! Oh my God! I was not expecting this," Gigi screeched, hand covering her mouth.*

*Lifting myself from the floor, I pulled her closer and tongued her down. Kissing her fervently, wishing that I would've waited until we got back to the room to pop the question so I could rip her clothes off and sit her on my dick. When we finally came up for air, I lifted Gigi's right hand and slipped the ring up her finger. At that moment I knew this shit was meant to be, the ring fit perfectly, no re-sizing necessary. Gigi silently examined the ring with a few tears streaming down her face. I gently thumbed them away. I hated that this pregnancy shit made her so emotional. Pre-pregnancy, Gigi was as hard as me and I felt like that aided in our close bond.*

*"I love you so much!" Gigi expressed after getting a good look at the ring.*

*"Alright Ziggy, that's all we are getting, add that shit up so we can slide," I announced.*

*"I got you. Congratulations. Just one thing, the ring goes on the other hand," he advised us and we both burst out laughing.*

*Young, in love, and just doing shit but that's why I loved her; Gigi was just as wild as me.*

"Rambo! My man, I got the ring waiting for you, let me grab it out of the back. Rambo's friends look around, it's the holidays, treat yourselves to something nice," he offered.

"Did that nigga say he got a ring? I know you aren't about to pull out a ring on Gigi tonight," Bishop interjected.

"You know he is. This motha fucka is about to cause a scene in the middle of game night and fuck up the vibes when she says no," Asim added, scanning the display case next to him.

"If you are going to propose again you gotta come hard. One night they were at the crib drinking wine and telling Ne'Asha how they got proposed to and Gigi's story wasn't comparable."

"The fuck nigga, you been drinking wine and gossiping with the hoes," I shot Saint a glare.

"Aye nigga, my wife ain't no hoe," Bishop barked.

"Saint, you saying my proposal wasn't shit, that's what Gigi said?" I waved Bishop off and addressed his brother.

"Nah, she actually thought the shit was cute. But I'm just saying. Bishop proposed in front of the new house he surprised Kalesha with and had Jibri help with the plans. Asim kept his proposal all the way under wraps and surprised Ne'Asha with a proposal during our trip to Vegas right in front of the Bellagio fountains."

"Nah, rub that shit all the way in, Saint," Bishop laughed. "Don't leave out how you took Ava to the Library of Congress and proposed during the cocktail hour thing. Don't leave that out."

"So what you niggas showed out, my shit still came from the heart," I retorted.

"And I'm not discrediting that but y'all need to get your shit together so you gotta do this right. It's affecting the boys and they are on track to really accomplish their dreams. I'm talking, entering the draft after their freshman year..."

"What you mean it's affecting the boys?" I inquired.

"Y'all didn't see their progress reports?" Saint inquired.

"Yeah, their grades were straight," I recalled.

"Nah, Pierre and Jamel both got a F on their progress report in math and social studies. It was a high F, fifty-seven and fifty-nine but still, they know the rules. That shit ain't gone fly if those F's make it on the report card."

"Those slick ass niggas," I grumbled, pulling my phone from my pocket to place a FaceTime call to them.

"Oh shit, y'all didn't know?" Saint questioned as the group FaceTime call connected.

"Wassup. How the trip going?" Pierre's happy ass greeted me.

"Fuck all that jit, y'all got F's on your progress reports? And lie, Saint two steps away," I snarled into the phone.

The smile washed off Pierre's face and Jamel's sneaky ass started stuttering, looking in every direction but mine. "D... d... dad."

"Don't stutter now. I'm glad y'all ain't getting shit until we get back. Everything we bought y'all going to a homeless shelter..."

"Nah, dad, listen..." Pierre started.

"Shut yo ass up. I ain't listening to shit y'all gotta say, just like y'all wasn't listening to shit your teachers had to say."

"Dad, I ain't gone lie, our progress reports were trash but that didn't truly reflect our efforts for the semester," Jamel asserted.

"Yeah, we turned all of our work in after we saw the progress reports. You can check online right now. I swear," Pierre stated. "Matter of fact, I'm sharing my screen so I can pull it up for you."

"Nah, I'll look my damn self. Ion need you slick ass niggas pulling no shit again," I declined, swiping their faces away so I could check their grades on the website.

Ziggy came from the back and I sat the phone down while the website loaded. He flipped the black box open and I smiled at the beautiful additions he added to Gigi's ring. When I purchased her ring over a decade ago it fit the woman I was with at that time. This upgraded ring featured diamonds along the white gold band, complementing the heart-shaped diamond. It perfectly suited the woman Gigi was today. Pulling the ring from the box, I took a moment to admire it, and prayed that Gigi would find it in her heart to forgive me, but that moment was short lived.

"I know you not about to propose to that chick you just met!" Jamel grumbled, reminding me that they were on the phone.

"Yeah, I'm about to call mama as soon as we get off the phone," Pierre added.

"Fuck no! Ion wanna hear shit from y'all until I see them grades on the website." I sneered, glancing at the phone and noticed the website was finally finished loading. Jamel's current grades were two A's, two B's, and two C's and I nodded my head. "Wrap that up for me Ziggy," I requested, placing the ring back in the box.

"Let me look at this tennis bracelet right here," Bishop requested, pointing at the display case in front of him.

Picking my phone up from the display case, I refocused my attention on the screen and switched over to Pierre's profile to check his grades and they mirrored Jamel's. "You saw the grades yet?" Pierre interrupted the silence.

"I'm looking now, and I'm still gone fuck y'all up. I just don't understand why y'all insist on playing on my top like Ion stand on business. I told y'all last time your progress reports were fucked up I was taking everything until the end of the semester and I'm doing that as soon as I touchdown. Stop turning y'all work in when you feel like it and meet the deadline. Now let me go before y'all fuck up my mood."

"But da..."

They started but I hung up on their asses. Wasn't shit to discuss, they fucked up and figured out a way to alter their printed progress reports with their sneaky asses, and now they would be staring at the walls after school and practice. Me and the fellas spent another few hours in the jewelry store while Asim and Bishop tried to catch up and pick out a piece of ice for their wives.

"God damn Asim, who blowing your phone up?" I questioned from the seat next to him in the Suburban.

"It's Mercedes dumb ass calling me on my business Instagram because Ne'Asha blocked her number last night. We don't have shit to rap about, she told Allie and Chloe that she was going to take them to Universal Studios today but called last night to tell them she ain't gone make it.

"Aw man again," Bishop blurted out.

"Hell yeah and I just had a conversation with her and asked her to stop telling them she's going to come. If she's coming to let me know and I'll make the girls available if she really comes so she can stop hurting their feelings and shit," Asim vented.

"That's fucked up," I admitted before taking Asim's phone from his hand after he silenced her call. "Let me block the deadbeat bitch on Instagram for you too." I offered, taking his phone because the buzzing was about to piss me off.

"How the fuck I ended up with the deadbeat baby mama out the crew is beyond me."

"I know, you'd think Rambo would've been more fit for that lifestyle," Bishop joked.

"Fuck you nigga," I spat back. "My wife and baby mama suit me," I bragged, flipping open the ring box to admire the piece of jewelry again.

"Saint usually show us up every year, but not this year," Bishop announced as we pulled up to the cabin.

"What makes you think that?" Saint laughed.

"You ain't buy shit out the jewelry store so your gift can't top this," Bishop noted.

"We'll see," Saint laughed cockily as he stepped out of the truck.

My nerves were in shambles but I was going to push through this shit. Our first proposal was some spontaneous shit and the wedding was even worse. We hopped on a flight after a big argument and got married in Vegas while drunk as fuck. I never regretted the shit either, we were engaged for nearly five years before we finally got married and it was long overdue.

Wrangling my wandering thoughts, I grabbed my bags and exited the truck with the rest of the fellas. When we entered the house the ladies were in the kitchen cooking and the aroma of fried chicken wafting through the air instantly made my stomach rumble. Stepping deeper into the house I ceased my movement in front of Gigi because I knew her. The slight smirk on her face let me know that she was guilty of some shit.

"What the fuck y'all been up to?" I questioned, eyeing Gigi suspiciously as the rest of the men greeted their wives with kisses and hugs.

"Boy leave me the fuck alone," she rolled her eyes.

"Nah, I know you. Your energy is off and that lil half smirk shit is something you do out of nervousness," I detailed, sitting next to her on the couch, grasping the hand that held her phone. "If it involves that nigga, I'm about to go hunt his ass down."

"Get the fuck off of me, Rambo. I didn't talk to that man, but I did see yo ass playing on my phone and pretending to be me to get him to come over here last night. He is a lil slow because he should've known that was a man texting like that but you... you one diabolical nigga," Gigi gritted.

"You did what?" Bishop questioned, his laughter filling the room.

"This ain't about that, last night is in the past. Right now we focused on what the fuck Gigi is hiding today," I squeezed her wrist tighter.

"Rambo, let me go!" She squealed but my eyes told her I ain't wanna hear that shit. Gigi's gaze shifted towards Ne'Asha, and naturally, mine followed suit. Asim couldn't see the slight shake of the head that Ne'Asha was giving Gigi because he was digging in the chicken she just pulled out of the grease.

"So all of y'all in on some shit?" I questioned, my head

tilted to the side as my grasp tightened on Gigi's wrist even more.

"You better tell them before I do because unfortunately my husband knows me like the back of his hand," Gigi blurted out.

All eyes were on Ne'Asha now and Asim stopped eating the chicken wing to question her. "What?"

"I told you if she stood them up I was gone whoop her ass," Ne'Asha shrugged, dropping more chicken into the grease.

"That's why the bitch suddenly blowing my phone up," Asim noted.

"So you unblocked her number?" Ne'Asha spun around to face Asim with her hand on her hips.

"Nah, she started calling me on my Instagram page. You can't be doing shit like that though, Ne'Asha. What if she tries to press charges? You have a business to run," Asim lectured, placing the chicken down on the table to pull her closer to him. "We are blessed to have you. It's not easy, especially with Mercedes moving how she does, but the way you stepped in and made them feel loved — it means the world to them, and to me. That's all that matters."

"I know," Ne'Asha confirmed, leaning up to kiss Asim.

"Fuck man, why y'all ain't tell me. Y'all know I ain't no snitch and I'm mad I missed it. If it's any bitch that needed her ass whooped it's Mercedes," Bishop grumbled.

"I thought we was better than that Gigi," he eyed her on his way out of the living room with his gift bags gripped tightly in his hands.

"Yeah and I thought we was better than that too but you was chilling with Rambo and that young hoe yesterday so," Gigi shrugged and I smiled because that was yet another sign that she gave a fuck.

Releasing the grip on her wrist, she pulled it back and

rubbed it gently before hopping off the couch. "Make that the last time you touch me this weekend."

She twisted off and I slapped Gigi's fat ass, forcing her to cease her movement for a moment as a smile spread across my face. Gigi peered over her shoulder and I blew her a kiss before she took off.

## CHAPTER SIXTEEN
### Gigi

"You trying to match a nigga and shit," Rambo eased up behind me and planted a kiss on my neck as I placed my diamond solitaire studs in my ear.

"I'm matching you because it's all you brought me back to wear," I grimaced.

Spinning around, I faced Rambo and he was so close that his Chanel Bleu cologne invaded my nostrils. His lips leaned in and pecked mine and I quickly gripped his lips and pushed him back.

"Put them on me again and I swear ta gawd I'm calling Law & Order SVU nigga. You don't have my consent!" I grumbled and he flicked his tongue out, licking the palm of my hand with a huge grin on my face.

"You mean that?" Rambo queried, pulling me closer to him. My breathing hitched as our chests collided and he emitted a hearty laugh before releasing the grip he had on me.

"Absolutely," I sassed on my way out of the bathroom.

I only had to share space with this nigga for another thirty-six hours then I'd be flying home to my own space away from him. Being near Rambo and his antics around the clock was starting to wear me down, it made me miss him around the house, and that's why I needed to get the fuck on asap. "You stand on business, Gianna," I whispered to myself while strutting down the hallway to join the rest of the gang around the bonfire.

Everyone was sitting around the bonfire sipping on their favorite liquors and I spun around to grab a cup from the house but Rambo was right behind me with two red cups and a bottle of my favorite liquor in hand. Rolling my eyes, I snatched the Don Julio Reposado and headed for my seat.

"Damn, I got you something to wear, bought your favorite liquor and you still can't offer a nigga shit but an eye roll," Rambo complained from behind me.

"Nope," I grinned, plopping down in one of the empty chairs.

"Aye, don't come out here with all that rah rah shit," Bishop warned us and I nodded in understanding because the girls were looking forward to the couples game night and I wasn't going to ruin it for everyone.

Rambo sat next to me and passed me a cup as Kalesha stood to announce the rules to the game as she distributed dry erase boards and two markers to everyone.

"Tonight, our first game is Mr. & Mrs. Wars. There is a bowl full of questions and everyone must use these dry erase boards to answer the questions. Everyone has a blue and red marker because the blue one is to write your answer and the red marker is to write what your spouse would say. Whoever has the most correct answers as a couple reigns supreme," Kalesha bubbled before reclaiming her seat.

"Dang, we couldn't just do drinking games like last year?" Asim questioned.

"What you scared you about to lose?" Bishop questioned him.

"Hell nahhh, I know my wife," he confirmed.

"Well since you talking so much, pull the first question," Kalesha directed. "And since y'all want it to be a drinking game too, if you don't get the questions correct, your spouse has to pour you a shot."

"Alright," Asim leaned up in his seat and dug his hand around in the fish bowl that held the folded up pieces of colored paper. It took him a moment to pull out a pink piece of paper from the jar and unfold it. "What's your spouse's favorite holiday movie snack?"

"This game already weak as fuck," Rambo griped.

"Well you can always leave," I retorted.

"Only if you're by my side," he squeezed my thigh and I didn't react this time. I chose to ignore his antics instead.

"It says what is your spouse's favorite Christmas song?"

We went around the circle and everyone wrote their answers, getting them wrong, except for me and Rambo. Shots were poured, jokes were cracked and everyone was feeling the liquor. Although we hadn't gotten any questions incorrect, I still sipped from my cup. The grin he wore upon realizing the score of three to zero would have convinced you that we had just won a million dollars. That smile, that panty dropping smile, was secretly enticing me again and I decided to lay off the liquor or else I would be laying on top of the business after the games tonight. Pulling the jar into my lap, I chose the next question.

"What is your spouse's favorite Christmas tradition?" I spouted off the question.

"Light work," Rambo blurted out before scribbling his answer on the dry erase board.

I was in the midst of scribbling my response on the flimsy

dollar store board when the silence was abruptly broken by Saint's voice. "So y'all just gone cheat?"

All eyes immediately drifted in Ne'Asha and Asim's direction because they found a way to cheat every time we played games. "Do you two cheating motha fuckas need to separate?" I questioned, placing my answers face down on my lap.

"Nah, we good," Ne'Asha giggled before taking a swig from her cup, I was just trying to see something.

"Man what's y'all answers?" Bishop questioned.

"Me and Asim's favorite Christmas tradition is watching Christmas movies," Ne'Asha bubbled as Asim flipped his board around for everyone to read.

"Man my favorite thing to do is buy you and the girls gifts and I thought your favorite thing would be opening those gifts," Asim read off his answers.

"I do love a good gift," Ne'Asha expressed before pecking his lips.

"Let me see your shit," Bishop grumbled, snatching Kalesha's board from her. "You think a nigga wanna decorate the tree on Christmas?"

"Yeah, I thought you enjoyed putting up the tree," Kalesha chuckled.

"No, I used to enjoy doing that shit with my young nigga but Jibri is twelve now. He don't be wanting to do that shit either, we both suck it up for you though," Bishop laughed as Kalesha pushed him away with a frown on her face. "Don't worry bae, I'll always be on that ladder prepared to break my neck trying to put the star on the top of that tall ass tree you got," Bishop expressed, pulling Kalesha back into his chest.

"Ava and Saint, what were your answers?" I questioned them, holding my board up against my chest.

"Ava's favorite Christmas tradition is staging the elf and mine is watching the basketball game on Christmas day,"

Saint flipped his board proudly and Ava stared at the back of his head with her face screwed up.

"I can't believe you thought that's my favorite Christmas tradition. I like watching the basketball game with you," she exclaimed, lightly tapping the board against the back of Saint's head.

"Awww for real bae? I love watching the game every Christmas with you," Saint turned to plant a kiss on Ava's lips.

"Alright, dysfunctional motha fuckas, y'all up next," Bishop nodded in me and Rambo's direction.

"We got this one," Rambo assured me, squeezing my hand for a millisecond before I swiped it away and held my board up.

"Rambo's favorite Christmas tradition is taking the boys to pick out families from the Salvation Army angel tree to adopt for the year. He said he gotta keep his boys humble," I read my answer.

"Facts," Rambo nodded and confidently spun his board around. "Gigi's favorite Christmas tradition is opening one present from me on Christmas Eve. Every year I buy the gift that I want Gigi to open up on Christmas Eve first."

A bout of nostalgia hit me and I reminisced about our yearly Christmas Eve tradition for a moment, completely oblivious to all the damn movement Rambo was doing until he was kneeling down in front of me. Black ring box opened in his hand.

"Gianna Auguste, look, I fucked up bad and I know it but we've been through a lot. Shit ain't always been sweet, but having you in my world made every struggle worth it, made that shit seem easy. I'm talking from the time we was jits, seniors in high school, sneaking into the movies because we ain't have shit. Then when we finally got our own crib and I was hustling just to make ends meet and yo crazy ass was riding passenger to make plays. Maaaaaan, when yo mama found out she wanted to fight both of our asses. She was right though, if I knew then what I know now I never would've had you nowhere around my street shit. Even when yo mama hated my guts, you was still down for a nigga."

Rambo's words sent memories flooding to the forefront of my mental rolodex and a toothy grin spread across my face thinking back on that shit. He told no lies, we were young, wild and inseparable. If my nigga was rocking, I was rolling.

"I ain't proud of the shit I did to put us in this situation and I promise when you find it in your heart to forgive me, I am going to make everyday going forward better than the last. We are going to grow old together, continue to raise these jits together and enjoy our last days together. I mean where else you gone find another nigga to suck that pussy when you in labor..."

"Nigga, what the fuck?!" Bishop groused as embarrassment shot through me. "Come on nigga, she got you down that bad?"

"Fuckin' right, she was in pain and I read somewhere that an orgasm would counteract the pain and they was taking forever with the epidural."

"Yoooooo don't ever put your lips on a blunt with me again," Bishop bitched. "You could've kept that nasty shit to yourself."

"You trying to ruin my proposal nigga? Shut the fuck up!" Rambo barked, turning in Bishop's direction for a moment before refocusing his attention on me.

"I'm just..." Bishop fake gagged before Kalesha nudged him.

"Well this really ain't no proposal because this shit until death do us part. You're mine now, forever and always. When you let me drop my jits in you, you consented to your death row contract. I said all of that to say that I'm done running the streets. Mia gotta run shit because nothing will ever come between us again. I put that on me," Rambo paused and patted his chest.

The sincerity in Rambo's eyes made my heart melt and the guards that were up quickly went down. My husband finally uttered those magical words I'd been waiting for, he was done with the streets.

"Gigi, will you do me the honor of planning and showing up to our vowel renewal ceremony? I wanna do shit right this time, give you the dream wedding you deserve. Kalesha's services have been retained for the wedding planning. Asim is already booked as the photographer and Kalesha even mentioned how you helped her with a wedding at The Tampa EDITION and you gushed over the place so I had her book it for our anniversary. Don't leave a nigga hanging in five months Gigi, marry a nigga again."

Tears streamed down my face as I said yes and Rambo's smile seemed to grow brighter as he slipped the upgraded ring up my finger. Initially, I thought Rambo bought me a new ring but taking a moment to admire the piece of jewelry, it meant so much that he kept the ring that I threw at him months ago and had it upgraded. Although Rambo was crazy and knew how to piss me off, he was always going to be ten toes down behind me and our kids. I'd never be able to replace that.

"This is what I have been waiting for," I squealed, cupping the sides of Rambo's face and pulling him in for a kiss.

"See, look all it took was for these niggas to come up the mountain to fix their marriage like Shiela," Bishop clapped behind us.

If I wasn't so engulfed in the kiss with my husband I would've laughed. For the first time in months I felt my world explode with love at just my husband's touch. We broke our kiss and Rambo stood to his feet, pulling me up with him.

Rambo drew me closer as if he was afraid of ever letting go, sending shivers through my body. I'm sure that our family was causing a scene behind us but I was engrossed in my husband, nothing else mattered. When we finally broke the kiss, I peered at everyone over Rambo's shoulder.

"Start picking y'all shit out because you are invited to the wedding," I bubbled before jumping into Rambo's arms. He instinctively grabbed me under my ass while my legs wrapped around his waist. "I love you so much."

"I love you too," Rambo replied, carrying me to our bedroom.

The angry sex we had the other night wouldn't have shit on the makeup pussy I was about to throw at my husband.

∽

We were probably up before everyone else because after Rambo blessed me with that make up dick, I ate and took my ass to sleep. I couldn't tell you if the rest of the group stayed out by the bonfire and finished the games or not because I had my man back. Dropping down to my knees in the shower, I took Rambo's hard dick into my mouth. I was a sucker for giving head and it had been forever since I blessed my husband with some.

Rambo ran his hands through my hair as I licked his length up and down, taking it deep into my mouth. The tip of his head played tag with my uvula until I felt his cum shoot off down my throat. I emitted a deep sigh as I looked up at Rambo's fine ass and offered him a smile.

"Get yo freaky ass up," Rambo grinned at me. Once I was on my feet, he kissed me forcefully, leaving me smiling like a teen with her first crush. If I wasn't so sore from all of the sex we had last night, I would've had him bend me over in the shower. "You don't know how much I missed you."

"I missed you too. Glad you got your head in the game," I expressed before finishing my shower.

When we exited the bedroom the rest of the house was already moving about the living room near the small Christmas tree that Bishop placed in the corner between the couch and end table. I felt terrible because I didn't get Rambo anything. My Christmas was supposed to be spent in Aspen with a whole other man. I went into the kitchen to grab a bottle of water then retreated to the living room to think about what I would get Rambo when we got back home.

Bishop passed Kalesha a card and she tore it open before smiling brightly at her husband. "Thank you! I can't wait!" Before Kalesha could come down from the excitement of her first gift, Bishop presented her with a jewelry box. She jumped out of her seat with excitement at the sight before her.

"What is it?" Asim's nosey ass questioned.

"A week long trip to The Meritage Resort and Spa in Napa plus a tennis bracelet," she bubbled. "My bae knows how much I love wine and a new piece of jewelry."

"Even if the ladies say your present was better you still ain't shit because you stole the idea from me but tweaked it a little," Asim exposed him.

"You ain't shit," Bishop laughed at Asim before Kalesha passed him a small jewelry box that he happily opened.

"Hopefully you'll keep up with this one," she mugged him as he retrieved the replacement wedding band from the box.

"I was gone get another one, bae," he explained.

"No need to replace it now since I already did," she replied.

"I appreciate that too," Bishop planted a kiss on her lips.

Ne'Asha passed Asim a medium sized box wrapped in gold wrapping paper. He tore it open, and exposed all of his teeth and gums at the sight of the camera in front of him. I didn't know what the specs I read on the box meant, but I knew that it must've been the cream of the crop the way he wrapped his arms around her and spun her around the living room while planting kisses on her cheek.

"Thank you Ne'Asha! I knew I wanted to upgrade my shit but I hadn't even thought about doing it," Asim confessed.

"I know, that's why I said let me do it for you," she bubbled.

He placed Ne'Asha on the floor and passed her two gift bags. The first was a tennis bracelet that mirrored Kalesha's and the second gift was a piece of paper.

"Ohhhhhhh! Me and bae are not going back home. We are headed to Vegas until the New Yearrrrrrrrr!" Ne'Asha screamed with her gambling ass. "Who is going to watch the girls? Do you already have that planned out?"

"They are going to spend the first three days with your parents then they are going to bring them out there to spend the New Year with us."

"You are so perfect," Ne'Asha cooed, rubbing his face before she pecked his lips.

Saint came from the back and joined me and Ava on the couch as we watched everyone else. "The best gift giver is here," he announced, passing Ava a medium sized gift box and a long black jewelry box.

Saint always showed the men up, so I was definitely curious to see what he got Ava.

"Open my gift first, my gift can't come behind yours because it probably won't compare," Ava giggled, passing Saint an envelope.

"Anything you get me will be perfect," Saint assured her as he tore open the envelope and read the message on the card.

*"Merry Christmas! I owe you a week of rest, relaxation and no*

*kids on a tropical island once your season slows down.* I'm looking forward to it," Saint smiled, leaning in to kiss Ava.

"Now open yours," he encouraged her.

Ava pulled the top off of the medium box and gently opened the tissue paper exposing two books. I took a swig from my water bottle because the gift wasn't exciting this year, he was always buying her books. Or so I thought until her eyes got bright and she screamed at the top of her lungs, holding the books to her chest.

"How did you find them?" She inquired, repositioning herself in Saint's lap.

"It took a lot of searching on international websites to find them," he replied.

"Well let us in, what the fuck is so special about the books?" Bishop pried.

"You see, I listen to my wife. She was looking for these books for years. She loved the story as a child but when she got older and went to buy the books to add to her collection, the author white washed the fuck out of the covers and these two beautiful black women were replaced by others; non black models that don't even fit the story. Ava refused to buy the updated version but the change was made so long ago that it was hard as fuck to find the original covers for her, but whatever my wife wants, I'm going to make sure she gets it."

Ava sat next to him all teary eyed and shit. Saint always found a way to show that he loved, listened to, and adored Ava, and I loved that for my good sis. With a tight grip on her books, she initiated a deep passionate kiss with Saint before she opened the jewelry box. I was close enough to get a good look at the book shaped locket with *Ava and Saint* engraved on the cover that rested in the box. Ava's mouth fell open and she opened it to read the inscription. *The day I met you, all of my dreams came true. I can't wait to spend the rest of my life with you.*

"Okay hoes, hang it up. Saint definitely won!" I cheered them on because my boy brought the effort.

"Hol' up bae," Rambo shouted, rushing down the hallway, garnering everyone's attention.

I glanced up at him as he ceased his stride in front of me. He passed me a piece of pink stationery paper and I squinted my eyes as I examined it. "Our prenup," I blurted out, looking up at Rambo.

When we got married, I scribbled one simple demand on a pink stationary paper and we both signed it after our wedding rehearsal. *Rambo promises to not let the streets take his love away.* Underneath my faded handwriting was a fresh set of words in dark blue ink in Rambo's handwriting. *Since you are giving me a second chance, I, Rambo Auguste, promise to never let the streets take my love away.* "I been walking around with that in my wallet since the day you threw your wedding ring at me. I promise I'll never do anything to dishonor our vows again," he assured me, plopping down on the couch, gripping my hand tightly.

"I know, cause if you do. That's yo ass!"

The gesture was so simple, yet it was all I really needed for Christmas as I snuggled up with Rambo on the couch. "I know you overthinking about not getting me anything, just give me some more head when we go back in the room," Rambo whispered in my ear.

"Let's go now," I replied with a smirk on my face.

Rambo and Gigi were back!

# EPILOGUE
## Ne'Asha

### *Five Months Later*

Tranquil—that's the best term to encapsulate the past five months. Since returning from our Christmas trip we attended an emotionally grueling family therapy session and navigated the actual process of going no contact with their trifling mammy. Allie and Chloe experienced their mother's neglect and indifference for longer than they probably should have. The pain of her abandonment was clear as they expelled tears and emotions like I'd never experienced before. It was heartbreaking for me to watch them go through that therapy session but we were a family and were getting through this new phase in their life quite peacefully.

Mercedes may not have had time for Allie and Chloe, but she did have time to press charges on me for assault. However, she swiftly changed her mind when Asim threatened to take her to court for child support if she didn't stop the bullshit. Never one to dodge her parental responsibilities, Mercedes jumped at the opportunity to continue to avoid financially supporting her daughters and stopped the bullshit.

After the holidays we bought the girls year passes to Universal Studios and they wore them out. Me and Asim had the unfortunate pleasure of knowing the park like the back of our hands now, and I was ready to explore something else but the girls preferred Universal over Disney now. Asim insisted it was time to loosen the reins and let the girls explore the theme parks on their own, considering they were fourteen and twelve, but the fear for my babies held me back. Plus they enjoyed our company anyways.

Like right now, they should've been relaxing in the other room with Jordyn and Savanna, but they were both standing on opposite ends of me in the bathroom mirror as I applied the final touches on my makeup. I swear these girls were like my shadow but I wouldn't have it any other way.

"She's about to ruin my fucking dayyyyyyyy!" Gigi shouted at the top of her lungs, garnering the attention of everyone in the room.

"It's okay sis, calm down," Gabby coached her.

The door swung open and their mother Gretchen stormed into the room. "What's all that yelling about?"

"The makeup artist isn't here!" Gigi stomped her feet.

"Look sis, this is her calling me now," Gabby raised her ringing phone in the air.

"I'mma stomp a mudhole in that bitch when she gets up here!" Gigi promised.

"Hush Gigi! The girl won't come up here if she hears you threatening her. "Beat her ass after the wedding if you like, I know where she hangs," Gabby expressed before answering the phone on her way out of the hotel room.

"Relax, Gianna," Gretchen gently caressed her shoulders.

"She was supposed to be here two hours ago, Ne'Asha already over there doing her own makeup because she won't have enough time to do all of our shit. Kalesha went into her room to do her own makeup. This day is already off to a bad start. Do you think this means I shouldn't go through with it?"

"Gianna, don't start," Gretchen stepped in front of her and held her hands. "I remember when you first brought Rambo home, with them big dookie dreads and all that gold in his mouth, I didn't like him. Then when I found out he was about everything I assumed he was about, I hated it. However, I grew to love him because I saw how much he adored you, that man will do anything for you and those boys and I love my son-in-law for that. Don't let the bullshit with that makeup artist ruin your day, today we celebrate y'all and I'm excited to see you finally have your big day. You just don't know how bad I wanted to fuck y'all up when you told me y'all eloped in Vegas. If y'all don't get married today I'll be the one showing my ass. Now dry your tears and sit down so this girl can do your makeup." Gretchen offered Gigi a bright smile before placing a kiss on her cheek

That heartfelt moment warmed my heart and I knew it left Allie and Chloe feeling the same because they both wrapped their arms around me. I pulled my girls in tighter, planting a kiss on the top of their heads. It's crazy how life works, I never wanted to be a mom but I was killing this shit with ease. In the future, I'd be in Gretchen's shoes and I just prayed my temper would be more relaxed by then so I could be as calm, cool, and collected for my girls.

**BOOM! BOOM! BOOM!**

"Open this motha fuckin' door. Who made my wife cry on our big day?!" Rambo's harsh tone echoed through the hallway. If I was the one who made Gigi cry I'd be hauling ass up out of here.

**BOOM! BOOM! BOOM!**

"I'll kick this bitch in!" Rambo shouted.

"Let me get rid of this fool before he scare the girl off and really fuck the day up," I offered. "I'll send Ava over to get her makeup done once I walk Rambo back over to the men's rooms."

Gripping Allie and Chloe's hands, we rushed towards the hotel room door with our robes swaying.

"Where she at?" Rambo tried barging into the room but I quickly pushed him back.

"Gigi is okay, the makeup artist is late but everything is fine," I assured him.

"Come on, you know she wants to do the traditional wedding thing, so you can't see her until she's coming down the aisle."

"Gigi, you straight?"

"Always. I'll see you at the altar," she cooed, and Rambo finally relaxed.

"Alright. I love you. I can't wait to marry you again, girl."

"I love you too."

"Alright, come on," I pulled him away from the room so we could handle business.

Entering the room where Rambo, Bishop, and Asim were getting ready, I smiled brightly at the sight of my husband. That fine ass piece of dark skinned man made a bitch want to sneak him back into our room for a quickie.

"Y'all look amazing," Asim gawked over all of us as he approached us in the doorway.

"Thank you daddy," the girls sang in unison as I silently blushed. The compliments never stopped flowing and they would never get old. When people talk about a strong black man, doing what he has to do for his girls, Asim was it, and I couldn't be prouder for how far we have come as a family.

"Y'all huddle together so I can snap a few pictures of my girls," Asim instructed, lifting the camera that was draped around his neck. I pulled the girls closer and we smiled as Asim captured a few memories.

"Allie, take a picture of me and Ne'Asha please. Once the

ceremony gets started and everything is popping off, I'll be too wrapped up in taking pictures of others to make sure that I have a few memories with my wife," Asim pointed out.

He came to my side and pulled me close. The scent of the Dior cologne I bought him quickly invaded my nostrils, further enticing me.

"Come on Allie, take the picture because I have to go relieve Ava and Saint of their duties so she can get her makeup done and he can come over here with y'all."

"Damn, why you acting like you don't wanna be around a nigga?" He questioned, turning me to face him.

I stood on my tippy toes to whisper in his ear. "If I don't get away from you smelling and looking the way you do, you won't make it to the suite to snap pictures of Gigi while she gets dressed."

"You got a point," Asim agreed before he leaned in to kiss my neck.

"I got all of that on camera, off guards be the best," Allie announced.

"Period," Chloe concurred, making us laugh before posing for the pictures. Life was beyond good, it was exceptional.

## RAMBO

"Aye Rambo, your wedding setup is weak as fuck, ain't shit out here for the real niggas," Bishop pointed out as I re-entered the room with Ne'Asha's assistance.

"That's because this day is all about Gianna. After all we've been through, I should've given her the wedding she deserved years ago. I told her and Kalesha to ball the fuck out and do their thing, as long as Gigi's happy, I'm happy."

"Mind the business that pays you, Bishop," Kalesha entered the room talking shit with Jibri and the rest of the boys on her trail. "And don't be in here showing your ass, I have a working relationship with this hotel. I don't need you to tarnish that with your antics. If there is a problem let me handle it today."

I waved Kalesha off as she approached Bishop to chop it up with him. If some shit went amiss today, I was definitely going to be the nigga to set shit straight. Our wedding was taking place at The Tampa EDITION, and I rented everyone in our wedding party a room for the weekend, so we were taking up an entire wing of the third floor. This was a family affair and I wanted everyone to be able to relax and have a good time this weekend. Plus, I learned my lesson from Bishop and Kalesha's wedding, if everyone was on site, nobody had an excuse to be late. I wanted Gigi's day to be stress free.

Scanning the faces of the boys in the room, I couldn't believe how big they were. Time was ticking and they were only getting older and closer to being on their own, away from our home. That thought made a nigga want to tear up. This right here was the only thing that mattered. We were all dressed in matching black three piece suits. My tie was coral while the rest of the fellas wore turquoise ties. Gigi decided on a turquoise and coral theme and I was with whatever she wanted. My boys had fresh cuts, so they were looking dapper as fuck as I scanned all eight of their faces with a huge smile on mine.

"Unc, the shirts you gave us yesterday were the softest I've ever worn. It didn't bother my skin or anything. I don't want to wear anything else from this day forward."

"Yeah, where can I cop some for him because that's all he talked about last night," Bishop chimed in.

"Oh you liked that," I smiled at Jibri. "Those are organic cotton shirts from Gap."

"Thanks," he nodded before claiming a seat next to Gideon on the couch and pulling out his phone.

"Alright, it's time for y'all to take your places so we can get started," Kalesha called out in the room.

Jibri looked up at his mother and she instantly mouthed that she was sorry for yelling, and he nodded his head. To say that Jibri came a long way was an understatement. Meltdowns were far and frequent. He attended a charter school with Gideon and my middle triplets Tyrone, Gabriel, and Gage. This was his first full year back in school since Kalesha pulled him out to homeschool him in first grade and it was smooth sailing.

Ironically, we were both embarking on new journeys. I enrolled in school to obtain a bachelor's degree in sports management. Saint was confident that my boys had a shot at going pro, so I was preparing myself for the next venture in our lives.

Kalesha lined the boys up, youngest to the oldest and my parents entered the room next, ecstatic to celebrate the day with us. Kalesha led us to the rooftop that she transformed into the perfect ceremony space. My parents sat on the front row and Saint, Ava, Ne'Asha, and Bishop filled the next few rows with all of the kids. Asim snapped pictures while everyone took their seats. While we waited for the officiant to make his way to the altar, I turned to my boys ranging from ages ten to fourteen and gave them a quick peptalk that I prayed would stick with them.

"When y'all find the woman you love, do right by her. When I thought I lost y'all mama, that shit was the worst feeling, y'all saw better than anybody else how sick I was. Don't be like me when you get older, be better than me, not all women are as forgiving."

They nodded their heads, even though both sets of my triplets were probably too young to understand, my eldest twins understood.

Kalesha came over and ordered me down the aisle just as, *I Do* by Rotimi serenaded the crowd. Off I went, swaggering past our closest friends and family members on my walk to the altar, grinning big as fuck without a care in the world. Taking my position in front of the officiant, I watched in angst as my boys came down the aisle one by one. The eldest four came to my side while the youngest four went to the side Gigi would soon stand on.

The song transitioned to *Spend My Life With You* by Eric Benét as Kalesha guided Savanna and Jordyn to the aisle, where they gleefully tossed the flowers. Turquoise hibiscus flowers and coral roses heavily lined the white aisle runner by the time they reached the end of the aisle and Saint directed them to their seats.

*A Couple of Forevers* by Chrisette Michele filled the distance and my smile grew wider as I spotted my wife, Gianna Auguste, strutting down the aisle in her white dress with both parents on her side. Gigi's smile mirrored mine, making a nigga's heart beat out of his chest. I wasn't nervous; I knew where we stood, and our bond was solidified. Nevertheless, this was the best day of my life, second only to the births of my children and a nigga was excited.

Gigi gracefully moved down the aisle in the white dress she had me travel all the way to California to pick up for her last week. It looked perfect on her, and I would go through all the trouble again just to have these moments. The closer she got, I became transfixed on my wife. Our eyes met and everything around us faded to the background as my memories were flooded with snapshots of our life together; I could feel tears stinging my eyes. I knew today would be emotional, but this overwhelming surge of sentiment brought out my emotions in a way that no vows or rings ever could have done.

"Asim, you getting this shit on film right? The nigga crying in front of everybody," I heard Bishop cackling from the second row but I didn't give a damn, Gigi had me fucked up about her for years and everybody knew that.

The emotions overwhelmed me as Gigi approached the altar, and her parents handed her over to me. I couldn't control myself; as soon as she was within reach, I tongued Gigi down. Technically, I was supposed to wait, but her lips were enticing, and I couldn't pass up the chance to press them against mine. Gigi indulged, and I could feel her arms wrap around my neck as we shared a passionate moment in front of everyone.

The rest of the ceremony was a blur until the officiant

asked that question that could ruin the fucking day. "Should anyone present have just cause why these two should not be joined in holy matrimony, speak now or forever hold your peace."

I released one of Gigi's hands and turned to the crowd and pulled my suit jacket open so everybody in attendance could see my new desert eagle resting on my hip. "Speak up, so I can clear this bitch out."

"Fucking Rambo," Gigi gritted, pulling me back to face her but I didn't give a fuck. I leaned in and kissed her gently in hopes of quelling her anger and it worked because she smiled again.

"Clearly there's no pressure so you can continue," I informed the officiant with a nod.

He cleared his throat and the rest of the ceremony went off without issue. We exchanged rings and when the officiant pronounced us husband and wife *again*, I pulled Gigi in and planted a nasty kiss on her. The start of our forever felt exhilarating.

**THE END!**

# FOLLOW ME ON SOCIAL MEDIA

Instagram: https://instagram.com/authorlakia
Facebook: https://www.facebook.com/AuthorLakia
Facebook: https://www.facebook.com/kiab90
TikTok: https://www.tiktok.com/@authorlakia

Join me in my Facebook group for giveaways, book discussions and a few laughs and gags! Maybe a few sneak peeks in the future. https://www.facebook.com/groups/keesbookbees
Or search Kee's Book Bees

## ALSO BY LAKIA

Surviving A Dope Boy: A Hood Love Story (1-3)

When A Savage Is After Your Heart: An Urban Standalone

When A Savage Wants Your Heart: An Urban Standalone

Trapped In A Hood Love Affair (1-2)

Tales From The Hood: Tampa Edition

The Street Legend Who Stole My Heart

My Christmas Bae In Tampa

The Wife of a Miami Boy (1-2)

Fallin For A Gold Mouth Boss

Married To A Gold Mouth Boss

Summertime With A Tampa Thug

From Bae To Wifey (1-2)

Wifed Up By A Miami Millionaire

A Boss For The Holidays: Titus & Burgundy

Miami Hood Dreams (1-2)

A Week With A Kingpin

Something About His Love

Craving A Rich Thug (1-3)

Risking It All For A Rich Thug

Summertime With A Kingpin

Enticed By A Down South Boss

A Gangsta And His Girl (1-2)

Soul Of My Soul 1-2

Wrapped Up With A Kingpin For The Holidays

New Year, New Plug

Caught Up In A Hitta's World

The Rise Of A Gold Mouth Boss

A Cold Summer With My Hitta

Soul Of Fire

Sweet Licks (1-3)

Riding The Storm With A Street King

Running Off On My Baby Daddy At Christmas Time

Crushing On The Plug Next Door (1-2)

Love Headlines

Gone Off His Thug Kisses (1-2)

Saint

Asim

Confessions Of An Ice Princess

Made in the USA
Columbia, SC
04 March 2025